THE GOSPEL
ACCORDING TO
JUDAS

THE GOSPEL
ACCORDING TO
JUDAS

BY BENJAMIN ISCARIOT

MACMILLAN

RECOUNTED BY

JEFFREY ARCHER

WITH THE ASSISTANCE OF

PROFESSOR

FRANCIS J. MOLONEY

SDB, AM, STD, DPHIL (OXON)

First published by Macmillan 2007
an imprint of Pan Macmillan Ltd
Pan Macmillan, 20 New Wharf Road, London N1 9RR
Basingstoke and Oxford
Associated companies throughout the world
www.panmacmillan.com

ISBN-13: 978-0-230-52901-4
ISBN-10: 0-230-52901-1

9 8 7 6 5 4 3 2 1

A CIP catalogue record for this book is available from
the British Library.

Designed by Peter Bridgewater

Printed in China

THE GOSPEL ACCORDING TO JUDAS is the result of an intense collaboration between a storyteller and a scholar.

The unlikely partnership of *Jeffrey Archer* and *Francis J. Moloney* was formed, after Archer had sought advice from *Cardinal Carlo Maria Martini* on who should guide him through this demanding project. Among his many past students of the Pontifical Biblical Institute, Cardinal Martini singled out Professor Francis J. Moloney, a graduate of that institute in 1972, who had completed his doctoral studies at Oxford University in 1975.

The project was as bold as it was simple. Archer would write a story for twenty-first-century readers, while Moloney would ensure that the result would be credible to a first-century Christian or Jew.

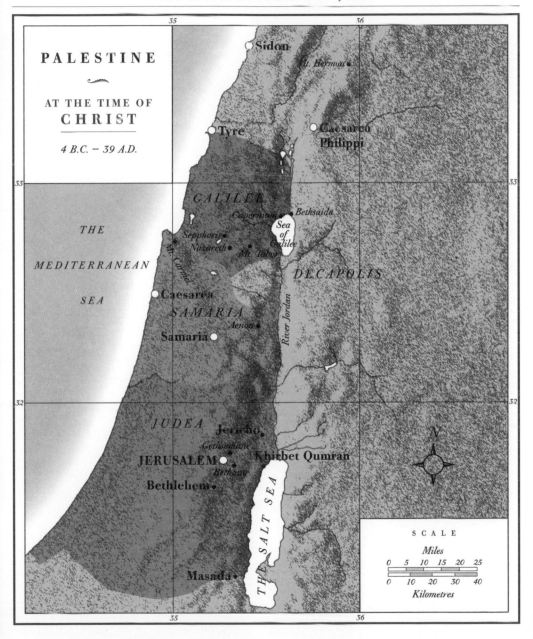

PALESTINE

AT THE TIME OF
CHRIST

4 B.C. – 39 A.D.

Sidon

Mt. Hermon

Tyre

Caesarea
Philippi

GALILEE

Capernaum • *Bethsaida*

Sea
of
Galilee

THE

Sepphoris
Nazareth • *Mt. Tabor*

MEDITERRANEAN

Mt. Carmel

DECAPOLIS

SEA

Caesarea

SAMARIA

River Jordan

Aenon

Samaria

JUDEA   Jericho

Gethsemane

JERUSALEM • Khirbet Qumran

Bethany

Bethlehem

THE SALT SEA

Masada

SCALE

Miles

0   5   10   15   20   25

0   10   20   30   40

Kilometres

JUDAS

CHAPTER 1

Behold the Lamb of God

1. This gospel is written so that all may know the truth about Judas Iscariot and the role he played in the life and tragic death of Jesus of Nazareth.

2. Many others have told the story of Jesus, recounting all that he said and did during his short time on earth.

3. Some were witnesses to what actually took place and they passed on, in the Jewish tradition of word of mouth, what they had seen and heard.

4. Others have written further accounts of the life of Jesus Christ, the son of God. These have come to be known as Gospels. [i]

5. One of those who were eyewitnesses to these events was my father, Judas Iscariot.

6. I, Benjamin, son of Judas Iscariot, his first born, listened to my father's account of what took place at that time, and have recorded accurately all that he saw and heard, initially in Aramaic – the language Jesus spoke – and then Greek, which my father taught me from a young age. [ii]

7. My father brought me up in the strict traditions of the Torah, and like him I have come to believe that Jesus of Nazareth was a prophet and a true son of Israel, but not the long-awaited Messiah.

8. Several other Gospels have recently been written, giving their version of what took place during Jesus' lifetime. But only a few of

them, not accepted by the new sect known as Christians, come close to giving a fair account of my father's actions during this period in

[iii]

our history.

9. The others do not begin to understand, or fairly record, Judas' passionate belief in and commitment to Jesus of Nazareth. Indeed, they have blackened my father's name to the point where he is now thought of as the most infamous of all Jesus' followers.

10. He has been branded a traitor, a thief and a man willing to accept bribes, and one Gospel even falsely reports that he took his

Matt 27:3–10

own life.

11. None of these judgments, mostly reported since the tragic death of Jesus, was made during his lifetime.

12. Some, determined to prove their case, have suggested that the name Iscariot originates from the Roman word *Sicarii*, which translated means 'dagger-bearing Zealot'.

13. Others have stated that it comes from the Hebrew *saqar*, denoting 'the false one'.

14. The truth is that the name Iscariot derives from the Hebrew *ish-kerioth*, meaning 'one from Kerioth', the town in which Judas was born.

15. My father's origins spring from the tribe of Judah. He was raised in Kerioth, a town mentioned in the early history of Israel,

see Jos 15:25 [iv]

loyal to the ancient traditions of the Jews.

16. The Christians continue to spread the word throughout Galilee that Judas was a man of violence, a hanger-on and someone who could not be trusted. Despite contrary evidence, these libels are still abroad and often repeated by the followers of Jesus, even to the present day.

17. Judas Iscariot was in fact a disciple of John the Baptist, and

willingly obeyed his command: *There goes a man of God, follow him.*

see
John 1:36

18. From that day, my father became a follower of Jesus of Nazareth, and was so trusted by the Master that he was later chosen to be one of his twelve disciples.

19. As a child, I listened to my father's account of Jesus' ministry, and later recorded his words when I visited him at Khirbet Qumran, shortly before he was put to death by the Romans.

20. My father has now returned to the God he loved and served so faithfully.

JUDAS

CHAPTER 2
Prepare the way of the Lord

1. Judas was a disciple of John the Baptist, and when the prophet first appeared in the wilderness, many considered that the prediction of the Prophet Malachi was fulfilled: *Know that I am going to send you Elijah the Prophet before the day of the Lord comes, that great and terrible day.*

Mal 4:5

2. John the Baptist lived just as Elijah had lived: *a man dressed in a cloak of camel's hair, with a leather belt around his waist and eating wild locusts and honey.*

see
2 Kings 1:8

3. Judas believed that with the return of Elijah, the day of the Lord was surely at hand. John the Baptist was the voice of one crying in the wilderness: *Prepare the way of the Lord, make straight a highway for our God.*

Isa 40:3

4. Many considered that John himself was fulfilling Israel's prophetic hopes, and must therefore be the Messiah. But he told Judas that he was not that man: *After me will come a man who is far greater than I am.*

John 1:30

5. John regarded himself as so inferior to the one who was still to come that he often said that he was *not worthy to stoop down and untie his sandal;* a task fit only for a slave.

see
Mark 1:7;
Matt 3:11;
Luke 3:16

6. Jesus was the son of Joseph and his wife Mary. He came from Nazareth to be baptized by John, who was his cousin.

see
Luke 1:36

7. Many stories of Jesus' birth and upbringing have been recounted,

but Judas always believed that Jesus was the first born of the lawful wedlock between his father, Joseph, and his mother, Mary. *Is this not the carpenter, the son of Mary and brother of James and Joses and of Judah and Simon, and are not his sisters here with us?*

Mark 6:3.
see also
Matt 1:25;
Mark 3:31–35;
John 7:3–8
[v]

8. Some of the stories about Jesus' birth that were being voiced at the time were nothing more than Greek myths that tell of gods in heaven who produce offspring following a union with women of this earth.

see
Gen 6:1–4
[vi]

9. Whenever stories of Jesus' birth are reported, all faithfully record that Joseph, his father, was originally from Bethlehem, the city of David, and that a child was born to his mother Mary.

10. These were difficult times for any Jewish family. King Herod ruled by fear, and allowed the Roman soldiers to wander the length and breadth of the land doing much as they pleased. It was not unusual for young women to be defiled by these pagans.

11. Joseph must have decided that in order to avoid any confrontation with the Romans, he and his wife Mary would make the dangerous journey to the remote village of Nazareth in Galilee.

12. In Nazareth, Joseph, a carpenter, found work among those building the great city of Sepphoris, while Mary and the rest of the family settled in the village.

13. It was while Jesus was growing up in Nazareth that he was taught the traditions of Israel by his righteous father Joseph, a son of David, and his mother Mary, a true daughter of Sion.

14. Even though Jesus is always thought of as a Nazarene, he was born in Bethlehem, the city of David.

JUDAS

CHAPTER 3

Follow me

1. Jesus began his ministry as a teacher in the lakeside village of Capernaum.

2. He taught his growing band of followers that the time of God's appearance in Israel was at hand, and that they should ignore any instructions given by corrupt local officials, *a brood of vipers fleeing from the wrath to come.*

see
Matt 3:7

3. Israel was facing its moment of truth, and the time had come to accept only God as the nation's Lord and King.

see
Mark 1:14–15;
Matt 4:12–17

4. Jesus' message quickly spread throughout Galilee, and people travelled great distances to hear him preach.

5. *While he was standing by the Sea of Galilee, the people pressed upon him to hear the word of God.*

Luke 5:1

6. He saw Simon and his brother Andrew, two local fishermen who were casting their nets into the sea. They had laboured unsuccessfully throughout the night, and were making their final cast.

7. Jesus watched as they pulled their empty nets out of the water.

8. He said to Simon: *Cast your net once again, but this time on the other side of the boat.*

see
Luke 5:4

9. Simon ignored the stranger's advice, telling him that he knew exactly where the shoals of fish made their breeding grounds, and did not need to be told where to cast his net.

10. Andrew remained silent as he gazed at the figure standing on

the shore. Unlike his brother, he decided to take the stranger's advice.

11. Andrew cast his net on the other side of the boat, and almost immediately it became so full that it took all of Simon and Andrew's strength to haul the catch on board.

12. Simon was overwhelmed by the stranger's authority, and leapt out of the boat and into the sea. He waded to the shore and fell at Jesus' feet.

13. Jesus looked at the two men and said: *Follow me, and I will make you fishers of men.*

Matt 4:19;
Mark 1:17;
Luke 5:10

14. Simon and Andrew left their boat and followed Jesus.

15. As the three of them walked along the shore together, they came across James, the son of Zebedee, and his brother John. They too were fishermen, who were repairing their nets and separating their catch after a night's work.

16. Jesus also called on them to follow him, and they immediately abandoned their boats and followed in his footsteps without question.

17. These four fishermen were the first followers of Jesus of Nazareth.

see
Mark 1:16–20;
Matt 4:18–22;
Luke 5:1–11

18. They gave up their livelihoods, leaving behind their families, their hired servants and all their possessions in order to follow Jesus.

19. From Jesus of Nazareth's early days as a wandering teacher, his authority inspired confidence and passion among those who gave up everything to follow him.

20. Jesus returned to Capernaum with his four disciples, Simon, Andrew, James and John.

21. It being the Sabbath, they made their way straight to the Synagogue in order to worship, and found the sacred place in turmoil.

22. A man possessed of a demon had entered the building, and

was screaming profanities and disrupting the worshippers as they gathered to hear the Torah read and explained.

23. Jesus walked towards the man.

see Mark 1:24; Luke 4:34

24. The man panicked, and started waving his arms and shouting: *Go away, Jesus. I know who you are, God's Holy messenger.*

Mark 1:25; Luke 4:35

25. Jesus, exercising the same authority that his disciples had experienced when he called them away from their boats, said firmly: *Be silent, and come out of him!*

26. The possessed man fell to the ground, and all around stared down at him, assuming that he must be dead. No one dared to approach Jesus, as they were fearful that he might also be possessed by demons.

27. Jesus bent down and took the man by the hand, and instructed him to return to his home

28. Some who had witnessed what had taken place turned to his disciples and asked: *Who is this man? And by what authority does he cast out demons?*

Mark 1:21–28; Luke 4:31–37

29. The disciples were unable to answer their questions, and news of what had taken place quickly spread throughout Galilee.

JUDAS

CHAPTER 4

Who is this man?

1. Jesus and his disciples left the Synagogue and went to the home of Simon.

2. When they arrived, they were told that Simon's mother-in-law was sick with a fever. Simon's family were fearful for her life, and advised him and his friends to leave quickly, as they too might catch the disease and possibly die.

3. Jesus showed no such fear, and asked to be taken to the sick woman.

4. Jesus stood by the woman's bedside, leant down and took her gently by the hand.

5. Simon, the other disciples and the rest of the household could not hide their surprise. They also began asking among themselves: *Who is this man?* Jesus appears to be a man of God, and has shown he has power over demons, but he has touched the hand of a woman who is not his wife, which is a public breach of Jewish traditions of purity.

[vii]

6. Jesus knelt by the woman's side and whispered in her ear. Even as he spoke, her fever was calmed and they were all amazed.

7. Jesus stood up, and quietly asked the woman to rise, which she did immediately.

see
Mark 1:29–31;
Matt 8:14–15;
Luke 4:38–39

8. *Later, full of joy, the family sat down with Jesus and broke bread.*

9. After resting, Jesus and his disciples left Simon's home and set

out for the village of Nazareth, a journey that would take them several hours.

10. When they reached the foothills that led into the village, they heard the sound of a bell, warning them that a leper must be near at hand. The disciples, fearful for their health and religious purity, held back, while Jesus continued to walk towards the sound of the bell.

11. As Jesus rounded the next bend, he came face to face with the leper. The sick man fell on his knees and cried out: *If you wish, you can make me clean.*

Mark 1:40–42;
Matt 8:2–3;
Luke 5:12–13

12. Jesus smiled, stretched out his hands and continued walking towards the man saying, *I do wish. Be clean.*

13. The disciples stepped forward cautiously and watched in disbelief as the leprosy deserted the man, and they were all amazed:

see
Mark 1:34; 39;
Matt 4:23; 9:35

Jesus not only drives out demons, but can heal all manner of sickness.

14. They repeated among themselves: *Who is this man?*

15. Some of his new followers remained uncertain, because Jesus had openly flouted the purity laws of Israel: he had touched a woman and healed her, and taken a leper by the hand and made him clean.

16. Could it be that this man, who brought hope and healing to the afflicted, was the long-awaited Messiah? Were they therefore the chosen ones who would accompany him on the journey to Jerusalem,

[viii]

where the Davidic throne would be restored?

see Mark 8:30;
Matt 16:20;
Luke 9:21

17. When Jesus heard them discussing these things, he warned them against saying that he was the Messiah.

Mark 1:40–45;
Luke 5:12–16

18. Jesus turned to the leper and forbade him to tell anyone the name of the man who had cured him.

19. But the leper could not hold his tongue, and ran into the town and shouted from the rooftops that it was Jesus of Nazareth who had made him whole.

20. Being heralded by such news made it difficult for Jesus to enter that place because the local people came out of their homes and surrounded him as he made his way to the Synagogue.

see
Mark 1:45;
Luke 5:15

21. Jesus' reputation as a great teacher had already spread throughout Galilee, so the leader of the Synagogue invited him to select a passage from the Torah and explain it to those who had assembled to hear him.

22. Jesus chose a passage from the Prophet Isaiah where it is written: *The Spirit of the Lord is upon me, because he has chosen me to preach good news to the poor. He has sent me to proclaim the release of captives and recovery of sight to the blind, to set at liberty those who are oppressed.*

Isa 61:1

23. Jesus looked up to find that all those present were staring at him in silence. Some had been told of the curing of the man possessed of demons, while others had heard about the healing of the sick woman, and even more had learned about the cleansing of the leper.

24. The leader of the Synagogue asked Jesus to explain the passage he had just read. Jesus' response was simple: *Today, this scripture has been fulfilled in your hearing.*

Luke 4:21

25. One or two of the Pharisees murmured among themselves: *Is this not Joseph's son?*

26. Jesus answered: *A prophet is never without fame, except in his own country.*

see
Luke 4:22–24;
Matt 13:57;
Mark 6:4

27. Others, who still wanted to believe, continued to ask: *Who is this man?*

JUDAS

CHAPTER 5

Are you he who is to come?

1. Jesus came to the river Jordan to be baptized by John, who had prophesied: *I myself did not know who he would be, and for this I came baptizing with water, that he might be revealed to Israel.*

John 1:31

2. After he had baptized Jesus, John proclaimed: *I saw the spirit descend as a dove from heaven, and it stayed with him. I had not been made aware that he was the one until God, who had sent me to baptize with water, said, 'This is my beloved son, in whom I am well pleased.'*

see
John 1:32–34;
Mark 1:11;
Matt 3:17;
Luke 3:22

3. From that moment, John was convinced that his days as a prophet of the Lord were numbered, and he told Andrew, one of his disciples: *I am not the Christ, I have been sent before him.*

John 3:28

4. Pointing to Jesus, he said: *Here is a man of God; it is time for me to stand aside and allow him to carry out God's will.*

see
John 1:29,
34; 3:30

5. On hearing these words, Andrew left his Master and ran after Jesus. Aware that he was being followed, Jesus turned and asked: *What are you searching for?*

John 1:38

6. Andrew fell to his knees and answered: *The authoritative teacher of the Torah prophesied by John the Baptist as a man of God.*

see
John 1:35–36

7. From that time, many of the disciples of John the Baptist became followers of Jesus.

8. Although John's days as a prophet were coming to an end, this did not prevent him from speaking with conviction whenever he taught the traditional beliefs of Israel.

9. He even dared to challenge the legality of Herod's marriage to Herodias, who had previously been betrothed to Philip, Herod's brother.

10. John proclaimed, for all to hear, that it was an adulterous union for Herod to marry the wife of his brother, even though the marriage had taken place after Philip's death.

11. These words, often repeated, angered Herod and, for his courage and faith, John was arrested and thrown into prison.

12. Despite having witnessed what had taken place when Jesus was baptized in the river Jordan, John remained unsure what God intended for Jesus of Nazareth.

13. While he was locked away in prison, John gave orders that two of his disciples should seek out Jesus, and when they found him ask: *Are you he who is to come, or shall we look for another?*

Luke 7:19;
Matt 11:3

14. One of those disciples was Judas Iscariot.

15. And when they found Jesus, he did not immediately answer John the Baptist's question.

16. But in the same hour Jesus cured many infirmities and plagues and cast out evil spirits, and to many that were blind, he gave sight.

17. And finally, turning to Judas, he said: *Go your way and tell John what things you have seen and heard.*

Luke 7:22;
Matt 11:4

18. When John the Baptist heard these words, he looked up to heaven and proclaimed: *This is the lamb of God who takes away the sins of the world.*

John 1:29

19. After this proclamation by John, Judas quickly retraced his steps to Galilee and sought out Jesus.

20. Once he had found him, he committed himself to his ministry.

21. Judas was inspired by his new Master, who taught with knowledge and authority. He was *unlike the Scribes and Pharisees,*

see
Mark 12:38–40;
Matt 23:2–7;
Luke 20:46–47
[ix]

who preferred to walk about the town in their long robes, and expected reverence when they took the most prominent places in the Synagogue, following which they made a pretence of making long prayers.

22. Judas was moved by Jesus' words and his interpretation of Israel's sacred texts.

23. After Judas had been told all that Simon, Andrew, James and John had experienced, and what they had given up to follow Jesus, he too wanted to become a disciple of Jesus of Nazareth.

24. Judas' faith in his new Master became so passionate, that he told everyone whom he encountered: *We have found the long-awaited Messiah.*

25. One of those to whom Judas passed on the good news was Philip, who was so moved by Judas' words that he also gave up everything to follow Jesus.

26. He in turn told his friend Nathanael: *We have found the Messiah, as foretold by Moses: Jesus of Nazareth, the son of Joseph.*

27. However, Nathanael, a pious and cautious man, was not immediately convinced that Jesus was the Messiah. He reminded his friend Philip that Nazareth was a village with no biblical tradition, and that there was no evidence to be found in the Torah that suggested the Messiah would come from Galilee.

28. Nathanael proclaimed: *Can anything good come out of Nazareth?*

29. Philip responded: *Come and see.*

30. When Jesus first saw Nathanael walking towards him, he said: *Behold a genuine Israelite who is without guile.*

31. Nathanael was amazed, and asked Jesus: *How can you know me?*

[x]   32. Jesus responded with the words: *Before Philip called upon you, I saw you sitting under a fig tree.*

33. Nathanael bowed his head and declared: *Rabbi, you are the son*

of God, you are the King of Israel.

[xi]

34. Nathanael also gave up all his worldly goods to follow Jesus, and because of his pious reputation, many others joined him and became followers.

35. They all began to spread the good news, telling everyone of the coming of a new kingdom for Israel that would no longer be occupied by the pagans from Rome.

36. Jesus did not openly acknowledge Nathanael's declaration that he must be the expected one, the Messiah, and therefore the fulfilment of the Davidic promise.

37. When they were alone, Jesus said to Nathanael: *Because I said I saw you under a fig tree, do you therefore believe that I am Rabbi, son of God and King of Israel? Much more will be made known to you, and far more will be required of you before God's promises are fulfilled. For the moment, follow me.*

see
John 1:35–51

38. Jesus made it clear to all his disciples that should anyone suggest that Jesus of Nazareth was the expected one, the Messiah, they were to be ignored, even denied.

see
Mark 7:36;
8:30 etc

39. Judas could not understand why his Master would deny his sacred calling.

40. He, like his fellow disciples, therefore continued to ask: *Who is this man?*

JUDAS

CHAPTER 6

Your sins are forgiven

1. Jesus, accompanied by his disciples, left Nazareth to return to Capernaum.

2. As he entered the lakeside town, vast crowds gathered around him, despite having told his followers not to talk about his good deeds.

3. Jesus set foot in the Synagogue where he had cured the man possessed of demons, and found another large gathering awaiting him.

4. The building became so crowded with people who wanted to hear Jesus speak that he could hardly move. Many believed that simply by touching him, they would be cured of their ills, even forgiven their sins.

5. One such group, hoping to bring a sick friend to see Jesus, could not even find a way into the building because of the number of people who wanted to put their requests to Jesus.

6. Judas was made aware of the problem they were facing. He advised them to clamber up on to the roof and attempt to lower their pallet down into the Synagogue. He even helped them remove some of the tiles that covered the roof so that they could carry out their purpose.

7. The sight of the paralysed man descending through the roof caused the startled onlookers to draw back.

8. Jesus walked towards the sick man, and on this occasion did not touch him. He simply said: *My son, your sins are forgiven.*

Mark 2:5;
Matt 9:2;
Luke 5:20

9. One or two of the Elders standing among the crowd were outraged by such blasphemy, and whispered among themselves that Jesus could not be a holy man because: *Only God can forgive sins.*

Mark 2:7;
Luke 5:21
[xii]

10. When Judas heard these words, he was unable to control his feelings, and shouted above the noise of the crowd, 'You do not have the courage to say these things in his presence; I say that it is you who are blasphemers.'

11. Jesus ignored the commotion caused by Judas' outburst, and turning to the paralysed man said: *Take up your bed and go home.*

Mark 2:11;
Matt 9:6;
Luke 5:24

12. The man stretched out his bent limbs and eased himself off the pallet. He then picked it up and walked away, as Jesus had commanded.

13. The silent crowd stood aside to allow the healed man to walk out of the Synagogue and return to his home.

14. As he departed, Jesus said to the astonished onlookers: *It is easier to say your sins are forgiven, but God has given me authority to heal and forgive.*

see
Mark 2:10;
Matt 9:5;
Luke 5:23

15. Most people who had witnessed the miracle were amazed and remained silent, but several of the Elders walked out of the Synagogue in disgust. They had been angered by Jesus' words, because what he had done went against their traditional beliefs.

[xiii]

16. After Jesus and his disciples had left the Synagogue, they started out on the road to Bethesda.

17. When they entered that town, they came across a man seated in the tax office.

18. He was gathering revenues on behalf of the Romans from those who had come from the Decapolis

[xiv]

19. Judas watched the man carefully and observed that he was not only taxing the visitors but also exacting an extra levy for himself.

20. Judas lost his temper with the man and shouted: 'How can you

take with one hand from your fellow citizens and then pass it on to the Romans with the other?'

21. The man made no attempt to defend himself and Judas walked away in disgust.

22. Jesus stopped and smiled at the tax collector, who lowered his head, embarrassed by his presence.

Matt 9:9;
Mark 2:14

23. Jesus walked towards him and said: *Follow me.*

24. Matthew immediately departed from the custom house and joined the other disciples.

25. Many ordinary citizens, seeing that Jesus was willing to include among his number fishermen, craftsmen in leather and iron, workers from the fields and now a tax collector, began to believe that they too could become followers of Jesus.

26. Judas could not understand and certainly did not approve of his Master mixing with such people. After all, it was not the way for a traditional holy man to conduct himself.

27. It was about that time that Judas was approached by a group of Pharisees, who observed that he was distressed by Jesus' actions.

see
Matt 9:11;
Mark 2:16;
Luke 5:30

28. One of them said: *Why does your Master break bread with tax collectors and sinners?*

29. Jesus overheard what was being asked of his troubled disciple and immediately responded by saying: *Those of you who are satisfied that you are healthy have no need of a physician, but those of you in need of assistance should seek out the one person who can help you. I*

see
Matt 9:12–13;
Mark 2:17;
Luke 5:31–32

have not come to call those who are self-righteous, but those who are aware of the healing goodness of God.

30. The wisdom of Jesus' words caused Judas to reflect on his own shortcomings.

31. He turned his back on the Pharisees, even more determined

to become closer to this man who was able to accept that, although he was a sinner, he could still be one of his followers.

32. The Scribes and the Pharisees were not pleased that Judas had rejected them, for they were becoming more and more fearful of Jesus and the influence he was having among the people.

33. At that time, the Pharisees only muttered among themselves, but it was not long before they approached Judas a second time, in the hope that they might convince him to join them and even turn one or two of the other disciples against Jesus.

34. Once again, Judas rejected them.

JUDAS

CHAPTER 7

The Sabbath was made for man

1. On the following Sabbath, Jesus and his disciples were walking by a field of corn, when one of the group, who had not eaten that day, plucked a ripe head of corn from the crop, rubbed the seed between his fingers and began to eat the sweet flour; soon the other disciples followed his example.

2. A group of Pharisees, who had been watching Jesus closely in the hope of finding some reason to reproach him for not abiding by the strict teaching of the Torah, said: *Why do you allow your disciples to carry out an unlawful deed on the Sabbath? Six days shall you labour, but on the seventh you must rest.*

see
Exod 20:8–11

3. Judas remembered these words, because it was the first time a Pharisee had questioned Jesus directly on his observance of religious law.

4. Jesus was not deceived by the Pharisees' attempt to turn this harmless act by one of his disciples to their advantage with such a narrow interpretation of the law. His reply was to the point: *The Sabbath was made for man, not man for the Sabbath.*

Mark 2:27

5. Judas and the other disciples were amazed that Jesus was able to silence these rigid guardians of the law with such simple wisdom and common sense.

6. Although the Pharisees were unwilling to come out publicly against Jesus, they were unable to hide their anger whenever they

heard him speak, as his teachings continued to undermine their authority.

7. They remained close by, in the hope that they might trap Jesus should one of his disciples break another tenet of the law. They did not have long to wait.

8. The Scribes and the Pharisees strictly adhered to the tradition of fasting and the Prophet Daniel had even risked his life to abide by the law.

see Tobit 12:8, Judith 4:9; Daniel 1:1–16

9. So when the disciples ignored the laws of fasting, the Pharisees took this as another opportunity to reproach Jesus.

10. They asked: *Why do you condone the actions of your disciples when they forsake the fine tradition of fasting that Daniel and John the Baptist always obeyed?*

see Dan 1:1–16; Mark 1:6; Matt 3:4

11. Jesus did not hesitate with his reply: *Can the wedding guests fast while the bridegroom is with them? As long as they have the bridegroom with them, they cannot fast.*

Mark 2:19; Matt 9:15; Luke 5:34

12. Judas was aware that the prophets, as well as the poets, had throughout Israel's history, often described Israel as a bride, waiting for the coming of the bridegroom.

see Hos 2:19–20, Song of Solomon

13. On hearing these words, Judas, along with Simon, Andrew, Philip and Nathanael, began to believe that Jesus might be the God-given Messiah, who had come to take possession of his bride, Israel.

see John 3:29

14. They did not voice this view openly as they knew it would further anger the Pharisees and might even place Jesus' life in danger.

15. The Pharisees continued to let it be known that they considered Jesus to be a sinner, a blasphemer and a man who broke the laws of the Torah. After all, had he not ignored the fine tradition of fasting, and now he seemed to be adding to his sins by claiming that he was the messianic bridegroom.

16. The Pharisees hung on Jesus' every word in the hope that they could find another example of his flouting the laws of the Torah.

17. The following Sabbath, when Jesus was in Capernaum, a man with a withered hand entered the Synagogue in search of him.

18. The Pharisees watched closely, hoping that Jesus would attempt to heal the man on the Sabbath, so that they could chastise him for a further breach of the sacred laws.

19. On seeing the man, Jesus approached him and said: *Stretch out your hand.*

Mark 3:5;
Matt 12:13;
Luke 6:10

20. *The man did so, and his hand was restored.*

21. This was all the proof the Pharisees needed to show that Jesus was a sinner and a blasphemer, willing to abuse the law, even in the Synagogue on the Sabbath.

22. Judas observed that many of those who had gathered to hear Jesus preach did not share the misgivings of the Elders, for they had come to hope that Jesus might be the expected Messiah, as promised by Isaiah.

see
Isaiah 35:3–5

JUDAS

CHAPTER 8

The rock upon which he would build his church

1. The Scribes and the Pharisees became so despondent about Jesus' growing popularity with the people that they agreed among themselves the time had come to take extreme measures.

2. Thus it was that the Pharisees, who held fast to the laws of Israel, joined forces with the Herodians, local Jews who carried out such orders that were decreed by their political masters in Rome.

see
Mark 3:6

3. Although the two groups despised each other, they were united in one common purpose: to rid themselves of Jesus.

4. Judas had friends in Capernaum who warned him that the Pharisees and Herodians were secretly working together to plot the downfall of Jesus.

5. Judas dismissed these claims, as everyone knew that they were sworn enemies, until he came across two of them whispering in the Synagogue. They parted the moment they saw him.

6. Judas warned Simon of his fears, and he in turn advised the Master to leave Capernaum until such ill feelings had withered away.

7. Jesus took Simon's counsel, and departed that day on the long journey for Nazareth, with only those disciples he had first called — Simon, Andrew, James, John, Judas, Philip, Nathanael and Matthew.

8. After they had travelled a short distance, Judas became aware that others were following them.

9. Some simply wished to remain in the presence of Jesus, while

others hoped they might witness a new miracle.

10. As Jesus made his way from village to village, the crowds grew larger and larger.

11. Whenever he appeared in a town, he would enter the Synagogue and teach those who had assembled to hear him preach.

12. Jesus would proclaim the good news, preparing them for the forthcoming reign of God in Israel.

13. He also touched those who were sick, curing them of their infirmities.

14. Jesus was aware of the injustices the local people were suffering at the hands of a foreign power.

15. Every town and village was administered by a group of corrupt Jewish leaders who were becoming wealthier by the day, while the Romans remained their paymasters.

see
Mark 6:34;
Matt 9:36

16. Jesus told his disciples that *the vast crowds were like sheep without a shepherd.*

17. When Judas heard these words, he reminded Simon of the prophecy of Ezekiel: *God would raise up a shepherd king, to restore the*

see
Ezek 34:23–24

kingdom of the first shepherd king, King David.

18. On hearing this, Simon responded with the words of the

Isa 53:4

Prophet Isaiah: *He took our infirmities, he bore our diseases.*

19. Simon and Judas were among the first followers of Jesus to believe that the promises of Isaiah were being fulfilled.

20. After Jesus had finished preaching in the Synagogue, he and his followers departed from that town and made their way up into the hills north of the Sea of Galilee and like a flock of sheep, the crowd continued to follow the shepherd.

21. When Jesus reached the top of the hill, the disciples needed to rest, and one or two of them were so tired that they fell asleep.

22. Judas sat on the ground and watched as his Master withdrew a short distance.

23. Jesus fell on his knees and began to pray.

24. As the sun disappeared behind the mountain, Judas also slept.

25. When Judas eventually woke, he looked up to find his Master still deep in prayer. It appeared as if his whole mind and body were committed to solitary worship.

26. As dawn broke, Jesus rose from his knees. He once again joined his followers, and began to walk among them.

27. Jesus stood on the side of the mountain and addressed those who had waited all through the night to hear his words.

28. He warned them not to gather simply in the hope of witnessing another miracle, and after leading them in prayer, advised them to return home to their families.

29. Jesus waited for the crowd to disperse before he gathered around him a small group whom he charged to remain with him while he continued his ministry.

30. *Jesus selected twelve men to be by his side. They were: Simon, whose name he changed to Peter, Andrew his brother, and the two sons of Zebedee, James and John; Philip and Nathanael as well as Thomas, who like Judas had been a follower of John the Baptist. Also added to the number were Matthew the tax collector, James the son of Alphaeus, Thaddeus, Simon of Canaan, and finally Judas Iscariot.*

see
Matt 10:1–4;
Mark 3:13–19;
Luke 6:12–16
[xv]

31. Jesus changed Simon's name to Peter, to emphasize to all his followers that he had been chosen to lead the other disciples.

32. The name Peter comes from the Greek *petros*, which translated means 'rock'.

33. Judas often recalled his Master praising Peter for his wisdom and insight, and on one occasion describing him as

Matt 16:18 *the rock upon which he would build his church.*

34. Judas was also one of the favoured disciples, and on several occasions it was he who pressed Jesus for a fuller explanation of his teaching and, when it proved necessary, was willing to take bold actions on behalf of his master.

see
Mark 3:13–15;
Matt 10:1;
Luke 9:1–2 35. Having selected his disciples, Jesus told them that from that moment, they would be invested with powers that would allow them *to preach in his name, cure the sick and cast out demons.*

36. As well as these twelve men, Jesus also gathered around him a group of women who had been loyal to him from the beginning of his ministry.

37. They had also sacrificed everything to follow him.

38. Among these women were Mary, from the village of Magdala, who came to be known as Mary Magdalene; Joanna, the wife of Chuza, Herod's steward whom she left to serve Jesus, and several see
Luke 8:1–3 others who were willing to support the purpose they all believed in.

39. *They gave both of their time and money.*

40. From that moment, until the tragic end of Jesus' life, the twelve disciples and the faithful women accompanied him everywhere as he went about his wandering ministry among the people.

JUDAS

CHAPTER 9

Whenever you pray, speak these words

1. Jesus and his disciples came down from the hills and made their way towards the Sea of Galilee.

2. By the time they reached the plain, word had spread that Jesus and his disciples had been resting in the hills and they were met by a large crowd who had gathered to await them.

3. Although Jesus had not yet set foot in the holy city of Jerusalem, on hearing the good news of his teaching and the many miracles he had performed, citizens came from that city and all parts of Judea to seek him out.

4. Others had travelled from the gentile coastal towns of Tyre and Sidon, while some had come from as far afield as the Decapolis on the other side of the Jordan.

5. Many came to hear him preach, while others, sick with infirmities, hoped to be cured of their ills.

6. Jesus walked among the vast crowd and made whole several who were troubled by unclean spirits.

7. Many others waited patiently, hoping simply to touch his robe, as it had become clear for all to see that power and goodness came forth from Jesus and that he transmitted healing and strength to all those with whom he came into contact.

8. One of those in the crowd was a woman who had been afflicted with a continuous flow of blood for more than twelve years. She

believed that *if only she could touch his robe, she would be cured. As the crowd surrounded Jesus, she leant forward and touched the hem of his garment. Immediately she was cured of her disease.*

9. Jesus stopped and said: *Who touched me?* The disciples could not understand what he meant, and reminded Jesus that he was surrounded by people on all sides.

10. Jesus again said: *Who touched me?*

11. The woman stepped forward because she feared Jesus would be angry that she had rendered him impure by her touch.

12. She fell on her knees, bowed her head and told him that it was she who had touched him.

see
Mark 5:25–34;
Matt 9:20–22;
Luke 8:43–48

13. Jesus said: *Daughter, your faith has made you well; go in peace, and be healed of your disease.*

14. This caused even more people to press in on him. When Jesus could no longer move, he gathered his disciples around him and, lifting his eyes to the heavens, began to address the vast multitude that had assembled to hear him preach.

15. Jesus said to them:

Blessed are you poor, for yours is the reigning presence of God as King.

Blessed are you that hunger now, for you shall be filled.

Blessed are you who weep, for your time of joy will come.

Blessed are you who suffer and are exploited, for your reward will be
Luke 6:20–22 *in heaven.*

16. As Jesus delivered these promises, a great uproar broke out among the throng, who began to believe that the long-awaited Messiah was among them.

17. Jesus waited for calm to return. He gazed into the crowd and became aware that a few among them were trying to stir the people into dissent, for they believed that such promises could only be

made by God and not by someone they regarded as a sinner and a blasphemer. But they were outnumbered.

18. When a hush eventually fell over the gathering, Jesus continued to tell them of God's promises:

Woe to you who are rich, for you have already enjoyed your consolation.

Woe to you who have more than enough to eat, for the time is coming when you will experience hunger.

Woe to you who simply live for pleasure, for you will soon mourn and weep.

Woe to you of whom everyone must speak well, because this only throws up false prophets.

19. These words caused an even greater division among the crowd and Judas watched as several people walked away in protest.

20. Jesus waited until the clamour had died down before he asked his disciples to gather around him all those who still wished to hear his words.

21. Jesus sat on the ground and, showing an abundance of compassion and understanding, continued to explain the good news of the forthcoming reign of God in Israel.

see Mark 1.14–15; Matt 4:12–17

22. Judas wept when Jesus told the multitude: *It is always easy to love those who love you, but it is far more difficult to bring compassion and unity where there is division. Be merciful, even as your Father in heaven is merciful.*

see Luke 6:33–36; Matt 5:46–48

23. Jesus then went on to tell the people that they should never condemn their fellow men, as there was no one among them who was not guilty of some offence: *Who are we to set ourselves up to judge others?*

24. As Jesus spoke, Judas repeated his words for he wished to pass them on to those who had not been present to hear the Master.

[xvi]

Why do you only see the speck in your brother's eye, while being unaware of the splinter that is lodged in yours? Beware of hypocrisy. For first you must remove the splinter from your own eye, before you can see clearly enough to assist your brother and sister in removing the speck that is in theirs.

see
Luke 6:41;
Matt 7:3

25. All those who had remained were visibly moved by such wise and compassionate words, showing how good and full of authority Jesus' ministry was.

26. Jesus then spoke another parable: *A good tree does not produce corrupt fruit, neither does a corrupt tree produce good fruit. So it is with us. Out of the heart of a good person will come good deeds, while out of the heart of an evil person will come only evil.*

see
Luke 6:43–45;
Matt 12:33–35

27. Judas, on hearing these words, whispered to his fellow disciples: 'From this man comes only goodness and mercy for those who reach out and touch him. We are fortunate to have found our Rabbi, and Master.'

28. When Jesus heard Judas' words, he turned to the other disciples and said: *Be wary of calling me Master until you fully understand my purpose and are able to live by its true meaning. Any one of you who fulfils this will be like a man who builds his house on a foundation of rock. When violent storms rage, the house will remain safely in place. But if you call me Master, and do not live by the words I have taught you, then you will be building your house on sand. So that when the storms come, as they surely will, your house will collapse to the ground. Consider carefully the meaning of these words, otherwise your hopes may end in disappointment. Be therefore perfect, as your heavenly Father is perfect.*

see
Luke 6:46–49;
Matt 5:48

29. After Jesus had delivered these words, he stood up and walked among the crowd, blessing those who had remained to hear him, before telling them to disperse and go home.

30. As they did so, Jesus continued on his journey beside the Sea of Galilee.

31. Judas, along with the rest of the disciples, followed the Master.

32. After they had walked a short distance, Judas boldly asked: 'Who is your Father?'

33. Jesus answered: *My Father is in heaven.*

34. Judas said: 'Were you speaking to your Father when you were praying in the hills?'

35. Jesus turned to face Judas, and said: 'Yes, I was praying to my Father in heaven.'

see
Luke 11:1–2

36. 'Master, will you therefore teach us to pray as you pray to your Father?'

37. Jesus smiled and, on turning to the rest of the disciples, said: *Whenever you pray, speak these words:*

Father, may your name be made even more holy on this earth.

May your kingdom soon come into this world.

Please give us enough bread to sustain us each day.

Forgive us our sins, as we forgive the sins of others.

Stand by us and protect us when the final day of reckoning comes.

see
Luke 11:1–4
[xvii]

38. The disciples repeated these words, hour upon hour, day after day, in order that the prayer taught by Jesus might be passed on from generation to generation.

JUDAS

CHAPTER 10

Give them something to eat

1. After Jesus had taught his disciples how to pray, they continued on their way to Capernaum.

2. As the Master entered the city, Judas was surprised and fearful when he saw a centurion standing in his path.

3. He said: *My servant has fallen sick. He is bedridden and unable to move.*

4. Jesus answered: *I will come to your home and make him well again.*

5. The centurion said: *It will be enough for you to say, your servant is healed, for I am a man used to giving and taking orders. I say to a soldier go, and he goes, and if a superior officer says to me come, I come. So my servant will be healed if you so command.*

6. Jesus said: *Return to your home and you will find your servant is well again.*

And at that time, the servant rose from his bed.

7. Jesus turned to his disciples and said: *I have not seen such faith, no, not in the whole of Israel.*

8. Although Jesus had instructed the waiting crowd to disperse and go home, wherever he turned, the multitude had increased in numbers.

9. While those around him were clearly tired and hungry, Jesus continued to walk among the crowd, showing compassion and concern. He turned to Peter and said: *Give them something to eat.*

see
Matt 8:5–13;
Luke 7:1–10

Mark 6:37;
Matt 14:16;
Luke 9:13

32

10. Judas wanted to tell the Master that they had sufficient food for his immediate followers, and that as they were surrounded on all sides, with only the Sea of Galilee behind them, he should instruct them once again to return home.

11. Peter also could not understand his Master's request, and warned Jesus: *We only have five loaves and two fishes.*

12. Then Jesus said to his disciples: *I feel compassion for these people. They have followed me all day, and I fear that they have had nothing to eat. If I send them away, many will collapse, and some may not even survive the journey. Do not forget that those who have travelled from Tyre, Sidon and the Decapolis are a long way from their homes.*

see
Mark 8:1–3;
Matt 15:32

13. The celebration of the Passover was at hand, and it was that time of the year when there was much green grass upon the ground.

14. Jesus instructed his disciples to organize the crowd in the manner Moses had done when he prepared Israel for their march from the slavery of Egypt at the time of the first Passover.

Exod 18:21–25;
Num 31:14;
Deut 1:15

15. The crowd numbered about five thousand, and they gathered around Jesus to await his instructions.

16. Judas recalled that the masses awaiting the coming of the Messiah at Khirbet Qumran had been assembled as the chosen people of God into groups of one thousand, one hundred, fifty and ten.

Community Rule
[1Qs] 2:21–23;
Rule of the
Congregation [1QSa]
1:14–15, 28–29;
2:1; *The War Scroll*
[1QM] 4:1–5,
16–17
[xviii]

17. Judas was aware of the time-honoured custom of the sectarians of Qumran, and began to organize the crowd as Jesus had commanded.

18. Once the task had been carried out, Jesus picked up the loaves and, raising his eyes to heaven, gave thanks.

19. He then instructed his disciples to take the loaves and distribute them among the multitude.

20. As Judas and his fellow disciples passed through the ordered lines, everyone was fed according to their needs, and when they returned to distribute the fish, no one was left hungry.

see
John 6:12;
Mark 6:43; 8:8;
Luke 9:17

21. When they had all eaten, Jesus instructed Peter: *Have the disciples gather up the fragments that are left over.*

22. The disciples carried out his order, and between them filled twelve baskets.

23. Judas counted the baskets a second time, because he could not believe they had fed five thousand people and still had so much left over.

24. While the disciples continued to collect the food, Judas reminded Peter of an ancient promise God had made to Moses: *I will*

Deut 18:18

raise up a prophet from among you.

25. Peter passed on this good news to the other disciples, and they in turn began to tell those around them that the long-awaited prophet, promised by Moses, was here present.

26. Jesus' miraculous gift of loaves and fishes, enough to feed all those assembled on the shores of the Sea of Galilee, gave hope to the many pious Jews who had been awaiting the fulfilment of Moses' promise: *And it came to pass at that selfsame time the treasury of manna shall again descend from on high, and they will eat of it during those years, because these are they who have come to the consummation*

2 Baruch 29:8
[xix]

of time.

27. Many who had come only in the hope of witnessing another miracle were beginning to believe that God's promises were being fulfilled in Jesus.

28. As the disciples passed on the message, a murmuring began to spread throughout the crowd that quickly grew into a loud acclamation as it was transferred from mouth to mouth, and then from group

to group, for many believed: *This is indeed the prophet who is to come into the world. Let us support him, and make him our King.*

see
John 6:14–15

29. But as Judas witnessed each new acclamation, he became more and more fearful. He reminded his fellow disciples that the Romans had orders to kill anyone the people of Israel claimed was a prophet.

30. He suggested that Jesus should tell the crowd to disperse, for he did not believe that this was either the time or the place for them to establish a messianic King.

31. When such figures as Theudas had risen in Galilee, the Romans had killed the messianic pretender, along with many of his followers.

see
Acts 5:36–37

32. But Jesus' compassion appeared to be limitless, as was shown by his next command: *Distribute the twelve baskets of food among the crowd, so that they may return to their homes without fear of feeling hunger or fainting whilst on the journey.*

see
Mark 8:1–3;
Matt 15:32

33. After the disciples had carried out these orders, Peter advised the Master that the time had come for them to continue on their way.

34. They travelled north but did not enter any towns as they feared that Jesus would attract large gatherings that would only impede his progress.

35. As they walked along the dusty roads, the disciples talked among themselves about the miracle of the loaves and fishes, which Judas was convinced proved the fulfilment of God's promises.

36. Moreover, Peter and the other disciples now believed that they were the chosen ones, and the moment was upon them.

37. But Jesus continued to tell his disciples not to address him as Master and never to refer to him as the Messiah.

JUDAS

CHAPTER 11

Who do people say that I am?

Mark 8:27,
Matt 16:13;
Luke 9:18

1. While the disciples rested in Caesarea Philippi, Jesus asked Peter: *Who do people say that I am?*

2. Peter was not sure how he should respond. Many of the disciples considered Jesus to be the Messiah, although not all of them had reached that point of conviction.

3. The miracle of the feeding of the five thousand and the many other signs they had witnessed were proof enough for some that Jesus had already fulfilled the hopes of those who had chosen to follow him.

4. However, Peter reminded the other disciples that Jesus always insisted they should not think of him as the Messiah, so they remained uncertain how Peter should reply to Jesus' question, especially given the political significance of being in Caesarea Philippi at that time.

[xx]

5. Judas offered his counsel, suggesting that when Peter answered Jesus' question: 'Who do people say that I am?', he should say: *Some say that you are John the Baptist, while others claim that you are Elijah, who must be sent before the coming of the Messiah. Many believe that you are a prophet that Moses promised to us long ago.*

see
Mark 8:28;
Matt 16:14;
Luke 9:19

6. Judas reminded Peter that a close link between John the Baptist and the figure of Elijah had already been accepted by most Jews. John dressed, ate and lived like Elijah, and therefore Jesus could simply be

fulfilling the prophecy of Malachi: *Behold, I will send a prophet, Elijah, before the great and terrible day of the Lord.*

see
Mal 4:5

7. The other disciples agreed that this was the response Peter should give to Jesus when he asked: *Who do people say that I am?*, as none of them believed that either John the Baptist or Elijah was the Messiah.

8. Judas also reminded them of the promise of the Torah: *I will raise up a prophet from among you.*

Deut 18:18

9. Although many disciples already believed that Jesus was the expected one, the Messiah, there were still those in Galilee, especially among the Elders, who refused even to accept that Jesus was a prophet.

10. The Scribes and the Pharisees were still encouraging their followers to reject everything Jesus stood for, and had lately joined with the Herodians to plot his downfall.

11. Despite the many miracles Jesus had performed, and his following among the people, even in his own ranks there were those who were still unwilling to believe that the humble son of a carpenter from Nazareth could possibly be the Messiah.

12. Some continued to ask: *Can anything good come out of Nazareth?*

John 1:46

13. While others were heard to say: *Search the scriptures and you will not find a prophet who will arise from Galilee.*

John 7:52

14. Even more discouraging was that some of the Elders were circulating rumours that Jesus had been conceived in sin.

15. The Pharisees, as well as the religious leaders of Israel, held to their traditional belief: *We are not born of fornication; we have one Father, God alone.*

John 8:41

16. Once Peter had answered the question: *Who do people say that I am?*, Jesus immediately asked: *Who do you say that I am?*

17. Peter, a blunt and at times impatient man, could no longer

hide his feelings, and responded with the words: *We believe you are the Messiah.*

Mark 8:29–30;
Matt 16:15–20;
Luke 9:20–21

18. *Do not express those beliefs,* Jesus warned his disciples, *even among yourselves.*

19. Judas was saddened by these words, but clung to the fact that Jesus did not deny that he was not the Messiah.

20. However, none of them was prepared for Jesus' next revela-

see
Mark 8:31;
Matt 16:21–22;
Luke 9:22

tion: *The Son of Man must suffer many things before he will finally be rejected by the Elders, the Pharisees and the High Priests.*

21. Judas could not understand why Jesus referred to himself as the 'Son of Man'. He could not recall ever hearing the Master use these words when describing himself and it went against everything he had been brought up to believe.

22. Judas then asked the other disciples if they had ever heard Jesus refer to himself as the 'Son of Man'. Both Peter and James confirmed that he had used this term earlier in his ministry whenever he

see
Mark 2:10, 28
[xxi]

performed miracles, or *when he explained with what power he forgave sins, and his authority over the Sabbath.*

23. Judas wrestled with the dilemma for some time before recalling the words of the Prophet Ezekiel, who had used the expression 'Son of Man' to emphasize the difference between the mortal prophet and God, who always makes allowance for the weakness of human beings.

24. Judas decided that the Master must have been alluding to Ezekiel, who had maintained that the God of Israel had chosen him, a mere mortal, to bring about His reign on earth.

25. And such was Judas' knowledge of the scriptures that he was able to remind his fellow disciples of another relevant passage from the book of the Prophet Daniel.

26. Daniel had had a dream in which many monsters came out of

the sea, bent on a path of destruction. This, Judas was convinced, symbolized the Roman Empire destroying the lives, the faith and the religious traditions of Israel.

27. Judas recalled that the symbolic monsters had later been summoned to the court of God, which Daniel described as *the ancient of days*, before they were finally vanquished and destroyed.

28. Judas repeated word for word the relevant passage from Daniel: *I saw the night visions, and behold one like the Son of Man came with the clouds from heaven, and was presented before him. To him was given dominion, glory and kingship, and all people, all nations and languages would serve him. His domain would be everlasting, and will not pass away. His kingship is one that will not be destroyed.*

29. Although Judas now felt he understood why Jesus had used the expression 'Son of Man', he was further perplexed when the Master later warned the disciples: *The Son of Man will be put to death in Jerusalem, but on the third day he will rise again from the dead.*

see
Mark 8:31;
Matt 16:21;
Luke 9.22

30. When Peter first heard these words, he said firmly: 'Master, we have no desire to accompany you to Jerusalem if it may only result in your death.'

31. Many others have written about what happened next, but Judas could never forget Jesus' words and he fully understood their meaning.

32. Jesus did not bless Peter in the manner earlier gospels have reported when he said: *Get behind me, Satan; you are not on the side of God, but on the side of mankind.*

33. Jesus' words, *Get behind me*, were used simply to remind his disciples of their calling. When he had first come into their lives, he had said: *Follow me*, which Judas understood to mean to walk behind him, for he was their Master.

34. Jesus was telling his disciples to follow him without question,

wherever he believed that path lay; this, despite the fact that he must have known they could not begin to understand his reason for giving such a command.

35. Judas also understood exactly what Jesus had meant to convey when he uttered the word *Satan* in their presence.

36. In the Aramaic that Jesus spoke when addressing his followers, the word *satana* means 'stumbling block', or someone who opposes the ways of God.

[xxii]

37. So when Jesus said: *Get behind me, Satan,* Judas understood his words to mean: *You are stumbling blocks in my path, preventing me from carrying out God's holy will, because your wishes only fulfil the desires of mankind and you fail to understand the ways of God.*

see
Mark 8:33;
Matt 16:17–23

38. All through the night, the disciples debated the true meaning of Jesus' words; in particular, his prophecy of a forthcoming journey to Jerusalem, where he would suffer and die, but three days later rise again from the dead, confirming the resurrection of the Son of Man.

39. Search as he might, Judas could not find any passage in the Torah that made an association between suffering, death and the fulfilment of the messianic hopes of Israel. He was greatly disturbed by Jesus' words.

40. When the morning light broke, Jesus called the disciples together.

see
Luke 9:51

41. He addressed them solemnly, saying: *My time is approaching. Let us set our faces for Jerusalem.*

42. Without another word passing between them, the disciples rose as one, and followed Jesus as he began his descent down the slopes of Mount Hermon and on towards the plain that would lead them to Jerusalem.

43. All the disciples knew that the Messiah would have to enter the

Holy City if he were to lay claim to the throne of David. But they remained fearful.

44. If Jesus had not warned them that he was going to suffer and die, they would have happily joined him on that journey with joy in their hearts.

45. At that time, Judas still wanted to believe they were setting out on a journey that would result in Jesus' messianic enthronement, and if it meant sacrificing his own life, he would have done so willingly.

JUDAS

CHAPTER 12

The Son of Man has not come to destroy lives

1. Before setting out on the journey to Jerusalem, Peter allocated tasks among his fellow disciples.

2. Following the role Judas had played in the feeding of the five thousand, he was put in charge of the common purse.

3. It became his responsibility to see that Jesus, the rest of the disciples and the women followers had something to eat, clothes to wear and shelter for the night.

4. It would be a long and arduous journey from Mount Hermon to Jerusalem, taking several days. Despite living simply, Judas knew that they would still need considerable assistance along the way if they were to arrive in the Holy City properly prepared for the Master to assume his rightful role as the expected Messiah, the Royal King of Israel.

5. Judas was also aware that during the long walk from Galilee to Jerusalem, they would pass through hazardous terrain, especially when they travelled into Samaria, *for the Samaritans would never share anything with a Jew.*

see
John 4:9

6. This would change if the Master was willing to impose his authority on those people who were proving to be stumbling blocks in his way.

7. Judas also had to consider the possibility of being attacked by bandits while they were on the road to Jerusalem.

8. These were desperate gangs of men who could no longer afford to pay the crippling taxes imposed on them by the Roman authorities. They had deserted their towns and villages and fled to the mountains, where they lived in caves and preyed on passing strangers, even killing them.

9. Judas feared that the Master would want to avoid any such confrontation, and take the longer, safer route, by crossing the river Jordan and entering Judea from the south.

10. However, once they set out, it quickly became clear that Jesus favoured the more direct journey, which filled Judas' heart with hope.

11. He assumed that this decision implied that Jesus wished to gather a large army on the way, so that when he entered the Holy City he could immediately stamp his authority on any non-believers.

12. As they approached the borders of Samaria, James and his brother John were sent ahead to proclaim the coming of Jesus.

13. However, the two brothers were disappointed to discover that the inhabitants of the first village they entered showed little interest in welcoming Jesus into their midst.

14. The Samaritans had no desire to alert the Romans to Jesus' presence, and then have their village razed to the ground for harbouring a false prophet and his followers.

15. James and John returned to Jesus and asked him to punish the Samaritans for their lack of faith. *Lord, do you want fire to come down from heaven and consume them, even as Elijah did?*

see Luke 9:54

16. Jesus disappointed them with his response: *The Son of Man has not come to destroy lives, but to save them,* and so they departed for another place.

see Luke 9:55–56

17. Judas agreed with James and John's judgement, and became ever more fearful of what might take place when they entered Jerusalem.

18. The other disciples carried out the Master's orders without question, and skirted the Samaritan village, thus avoiding any confrontation with its inhabitants.

19. A small band of followers came out of the village to join Jesus, but they numbered only a few.

20. That evening, while others ate and rested, Jesus stole away and with calm intensity immersed himself in prayer.

[xxiii] 21. When Judas knelt near his Master, he heard Jesus utter the word *Abba*.

22. This gave Judas renewed confidence that Jesus truly was the son of God, though he still could not understand why the Master continued to call himself the *Son of Man*.

23. Why was Jesus prophesying that he would die soon after he entered Jerusalem and then three days later rise from the dead, finally to be restored to his followers, before taking his place on the right hand of God?

24. Judas continued to pray that God would give Jesus the means to overthrow his enemies when they entered Jerusalem, and establish him as the Davidic King in Israel.

JUDAS

CHAPTER 13

Take up the cross and follow me

1. When the sun rose the following morning, Jesus and his growing band continued on their journey south to Jerusalem.

2. As they entered the city of Aenon, they were met by a large crowd who wanted to join Jesus on his triumphal march.

3. Among those who gathered around him was a rich young man who owned several leagues of land, reared vast flocks and commanded a large household of servants.

4. Judas made himself known to him.

5. The rich young man made it clear that if Jesus were to assure him of some important position once he had established himself as the King of Israel, he would willingly sacrifice his entire wealth to follow him.

6. Judas, aware of how the rich young man could assist their purpose, took him directly to the Master, who welcomed him with open arms.

7. The young man, encouraged by Jesus' gesture, said: *Good Rabbi, are you going to establish God's kingdom in Israel?*

8. Jesus smiled. *Why do you call me good? No one is good but God alone.*

Mark 10:18; Luke 18:19

9. Judas was delighted by the Master's response because, as a devout Jew, he did not, as some Greeks did, wish to make Jesus a God. This was not the way of a true son of Israel. There was only one God,

YHWH, and the Messiah was the expected messenger of God, but not God himself.

10. The young man, heartened by this reply, enquired boldly if he might join Jesus as one of his disciples.

11. Jesus said: *Yes, but first you must obey the commandments of God.*

12. *And what are they?*

13. *Do not kill. Do not commit adultery. Do not steal. Do not bear false witness. Do not defraud. Honour your father and your mother.*

14. The rich young man was perplexed, for he had been taught to believe that Moses had handed down ten commandments. *Teacher, I have observed all the commandments from the time I was a small child.*

15. Jesus smiled and aware that he was a devout man, agreed that he could become a disciple.

16. The young man was overwhelmed, and assured Judas that he was willing to give up everything to follow the Master.

see
Mark 10:21;
Matt 19:21;
Luke 18:22

17. Jesus, on hearing these words, said: *Go and sell all that you have, and give it to the poor. Once you have done that, you will have treasure enough in heaven, and come take up the cross and follow me.*

18. Judas became distressed, aware that if Jesus hoped to establish himself as the expected Son of David, the Messiah and King of Israel, he could not hope to do so as a wandering prophet who rejected such a generous offer. Worse, he had commanded the rich young man to sell everything he possessed and distribute his wealth among the poor, which was not in keeping with the best traditions of Israel.

19. Throughout Israel's history, God's glory had always been measured by the wealth and success of the nation.

20. When David was King, the Jews occupied many lands, produced abundant crops and their flocks were ever bountiful. This was only true while the city was ruled over by a powerful king, who

was respected and feared by those who lived in the surrounding countries.

21. Judas had been taught to believe that during that time Israel was in true communion with God. He hoped and expected Jesus would restore that enviable position.

22. Had not Solomon sung in tribute to a great king:

Long may he live!
May gold of Sheba be given to him.
May prayer be made for him continually,
and blessings invoked for him all day long.
May there be an abundance of grain in the land;
may it wave on the tops of the mountains;
may its fruits be like Lebanon;
and may people flourish in the cities
like the grass in the field.
May his name endure forever,
his fame continue as long as the sun.
May all nations be blessed in him;
And the whole earth be filled with his glory.

Psalm 72:15–17
for Solomon

23. Judas was in despair as the rich young man walked away.

24. The rich young man's only response: *You have chosen to follow a dangerous man, who will lead to the fall of many in Israel.*

see
Luke 2:34

JUDAS

CHAPTER 14

You are people of little faith

1. As Jesus' bedraggled band of followers drifted south towards Jericho, Judas warned Peter that the coffers were running low and that the Master should be informed.

2. Peter refused to pass on such bad news and told Judas to carry out the Master's bidding without question.

3. Although Judas was in despair his spirits were raised once again when Jesus was approached by a generous and devout Scribe, skilled in the interpretation of the laws of Israel. He said to Jesus: *Master, I will follow you wherever you go.*

see
Matt 8:19–20;
Luke 9:57–58
4. But Jesus said: *Foxes have holes and birds of the air have nests, but the Son of Man has nowhere to lay his head.*

5. The Scribe was not able to comprehend what Jesus meant by this reference to the 'Son of Man', and departed that place.

6. Another came to Jesus and said: *I wish to follow you, but first I must return to Galilee and bury my father.*

see
Matt 8:21–22
7. Judas was astonished when the Master said: *Follow me, and leave the dead to bury their dead.*

8. Everyone who heard these words knew that it was a sacred duty for any son of Israel to bury his father, as the family is the centre of Jewish life and the father its head.

9. The man left Jesus and departed for Galilee.

10. Judas demanded of Peter: 'Did not Moses include among the

Ten Commandments passed down by God at Sinai: *Honour your father and your mother so that you may live long in the land that YHWH your God is giving you?'*

Exod 20:12

11. But Peter ignored him, and continued to remind his fellow disciples of the true meaning of Jesus' warning, *Get behind me, Satan,* which only made Judas more fearful.

12. Jesus, aware of what was passing through their minds, gath- ered the disciples together and said: *Why are you afraid? You are people of little faith.*

see Matt 8:26; see Mark 4:40–41; Luke 8:25

13. Judas could not understand why Jesus was challenging them in this manner; had they not proved their commitment a thousand- fold? Had they ever questioned his authority?

14. By the evening of the third day, Jesus and his followers had reached the slopes of Mount Tabor, and were preparing to rest before nightfall.

[xxiv]

15. Judas was distributing food and blankets in preparation for the cold night ahead, when he saw Jesus take Peter, James and John to one side.

see Matt 17:1

16. Without explanation, the four of them began to ascend the long, steep slope up the mountain.

17. Judas and the other disciples fell asleep, and did not wake again until dawn, when they found Jesus walking among them. He said: *Let us rest a little longer, before we set out on the next part of our journey.*

see Mark 6:31

18. Judas observed that Peter, James and John were whispering among themselves.

19. He approached Peter and said: 'What took place when you were with Jesus on the mountain?'

20. Peter was unable to hide his joy, and although the Master had instructed them not to reveal what had happened on the mountain,

he hesitated only for a moment:

I saw a powerful light, and before me appeared figures from Israel's past, and they spoke to Jesus, and the skies opened and a voice said, 'This is my beloved Son, listen to his words.'

21. Peter went on to tell Judas: 'I understand what awaits us when we travel to Jerusalem, and I now accept that Jesus will rise from the dead.'

see
Mark 9:9–13;
Matt 17:9–13

22. Judas left him for he was inconsolable. If Jesus was the expected Davidic Messiah, the King of Israel, why would he enter Jerusalem only to be slain, and then to rise again from the dead three days later? There was nothing written or spoken in Jewish tradition that suggested such a happening would take place.

23. But it was clear to Judas that the thought of Jesus' death no longer alarmed Peter, James or John, who had clearly been overwhelmed by what they had seen on the mountain during the night.

24. For the first time, Judas began to doubt that Jesus, in whom he had placed so much faith and commitment, was the Messiah Israel had been waiting for.

25. Judas withdrew from his fellow disciples and kept his own counsel.

26. When the sun reached its zenith, Jesus stopped to rest and gathered around him all his followers. He addressed them with these words: *The Son of Man will be given into the hands of men, and they will kill him. But God will not abandon him. He will live again with you on the other side of death.*

see
Mark 9:31;
Matt 17:22–23;
Luke 9:44
[xxv]

27. Judas loved the Master above all men, and after John the Baptist had commanded: *There goes a man of God, follow him,* he had become wholly committed to Jesus' ministry.

see
John 1:34–36

28. But Judas was also a devout son of Israel, who looked to Jesus

to fulfil the prophecies of Israel's sages, and now feared that this Son of Man had no intention of entering Jerusalem with authority to reclaim the Davidic throne of Israel for the Jewish people.

29. Judas felt a deep pain in his heart while he pondered these matters, aware that if Jesus were to continue on this course, then all would be lost. Once again the Romans must triumph and the very survival of Israel might be threatened.

JUDAS

CHAPTER 15

You have chosen to follow a dangerous man

1. Jesus and his disciples were approaching the end of their journey to Jerusalem.

2. They planned to spend nightfall in Jericho before ascending the slopes of Judea and finally entering the Holy City.

3. They passed through the gates of Jericho during the early evening, to find the vendors in the market place closing their booths, while the labourers who had been toiling in the fields were wending their way home.

4. As Jesus walked through the streets, the local people gathered [xxvi] around him, curious to set eyes on the stranger from Galilee.

5. Rumours of a new prophet, possibly even the Messiah, had reached Jericho some time before Jesus appeared. Like so many devout Jews, the citizens of Jericho lived in hope that someone had finally come to rescue them from the tyranny of Rome.

6. As Jesus progressed through the streets, some simply stopped to gaze at the man from Nazareth, *while others greeted him with cries of Master, Rabbi, even Messiah, but Jesus continued on his way without responding to the exhortations of the noisy crowd.*

7. Judas left his Master to go in search of lodgings where Jesus and the other disciples might lay their heads for the night. He searched in vain, as there were no longer enough coins left in the common purse to cover such an expense, if he were also to purchase sufficient

food so that they might eat.

8. Judas returned empty-handed, to find Jesus surrounded by many new followers, as he continued his slow progress through the streets of Jericho.

9. Suddenly, without warning, Jesus stopped. He looked up into a sycamore tree and saw, perched in its branches, Zacchaeus, the city's chief tax collector.

10. Zacchaeus, a corrupt man in the pay of the Romans, *was despised by his fellow Jews, not only for being a sinner, but also because of his tiny stature.*

11. The startled man peered down at Jesus. A hush fell upon the crowd as they waited for Jesus to mock him. After all, the tax collector had made his fortune as a Roman lackey and was now surrounded by a hostile crowd, allowing him no visible means of escape.

12. The crowd began to jeer, and only fell silent again when Jesus raised his hands in greeting and said: *Zacchaeus, make haste and come down, for I must abide in your home tonight.*

13. Zacchaeus scrambled down from the branches of the tree and joined Jesus as he stood among the crowd.

14. Judas looked on in disbelief as Jesus embraced a man who had been shunned by his fellow Jews, and worse, he now intended to spend the night under the man's roof.

15. Zacchaeus was so overcome by Jesus' compassion that he declared to a startled crowd: *Behold, Lord, the half of my possessions I give to the poor; and if I have defrauded any man, I will return it to him, fourfold.*

16. The local people greeted this offer with loud acclamation. They then allowed Zacchaeus to run on ahead to his house so that he could warn his servants that Jesus and his disciples would be

guests in his home that night.

17. Judas could not understand why his Master had commanded the rich young man to part with all his goods and distribute his wealth among the poor, while allowing Zacchaeus to retain half of his wealth.

18. Peter could offer no explanation, and was also puzzled as to why Jesus was willing to rest his head in the home of a man who had been banned from the Synagogue for his public sins.

19. The crowd that engulfed Jesus was equally bemused. The majority looked on in silence, while some burst out laughing and others turned their backs on him.

20. Jesus left them to make his way to the home of Zacchaeus, while Judas and the other disciples followed reluctantly in his wake.

21. When Jesus first entered the tax collector's home, he addressed the startled servants with the words: *Today salvation has come to this* Luke 19:2–9 *house, since he is also a son of Abraham.*

22. Judas was outraged that his Master could mention Abraham and Zacchaeus in the same breath. Was not one the father of the nation, while the other remained a despised sinner?

23. After they had broken bread, Jesus spoke to his disciples. He warned them yet again that his time was nigh, for he was about to *see* return to his Father, but after three days he would rise again from the Matt 26:1; John 13:1 dead and once more come among them.

24. Judas was disheartened by Jesus' speaking of his own death, but did not at that time press the Master for an explanation.

25. Judas was unable to sleep that night while he remained under the roof of an impure man who owed his wealth and position to a race of disbelievers.

26. While others slept, Judas wrestled with the multitude of problems Jesus had revisited.

27. Since they had descended from Mount Tabor, the Master's actions had not been those of a messianic leader intent on entering Jerusalem in triumph to claim the Davidic throne of Israel.

28. Without an army to support him, Judas was fearful of what might happen to the Master when he finally entered the Holy City.

29. So many of Jesus' enemies, among them the Elders and Pharisees, would be looking for the slightest excuse to discredit him, even destroy him.

30. Judas recalled the exhilaration he had felt when he had first joined Jesus' band of followers. He had been overwhelmed by the authority of the Master's teaching and proud to be numbered among the chosen twelve.

31. But would he now have to accept that Jesus was no more than a prophet, and that the rich young man might turn out to be right when he had warned: *You have chosen to follow a dangerous man, who will lead to the fall of many in Israel?*

see
Luke 2:34
[xxvii]

JUDAS

CHAPTER 16

Go your way and do likewise

1. They could hear him long before they could see him.

2. Blind Bartimaeus sat begging on the same street corner every day, from the moment the sun rose until it fell.

3. As Jesus left Jericho that morning Bartimaeus' cry differed from the one he had always uttered in the past, and Judas assumed that the Master would reject him: *Jesus, Son of David, have mercy on me.*

4. Peter ran ahead of Jesus, aware that the Master had instructed the disciples not to allow anyone to call him: *Son of David.*

5. He ordered the beggar to hold his tongue.

6. But Bartimaeus, aware that Jesus must therefore be close at hand, cried even louder: *Jesus, Son of David, have mercy on me.*

7. When Jesus heard these words, he said: *Call him.*

8. Andrew came to Bartimaeus' side, helped him up and led the blind man to Jesus. Bartimaeus fell on his knees.

9. Jesus looked down at the blind man and said with compassion, *What do you expect of me?*

10. Bartimaeus raised his head and said: *Lord, let me have my sight.*

see
Matt 20:30–32;
Mark 10:47–52;
Luke 18:38–42
11. Jesus touched his tongue and then rubbed the spittle on Bartimaeus' eyes, saying: *Go your way, your faith has healed you.*

12. Judas' heart was filled with renewed expectation. A blind beggar had called Jesus *Son of David* and the Master had not denied his words.

[xxviii]
13. Was this at last the sign that Jesus now accepted, a short time

before they would enter the Holy City, that he was the Messiah and would make YHWH absolute ruler and King?

14. A devout Scribe from Jerusalem left the Holy City to seek out Jesus, for he had heard some say that the son of a carpenter from Nazareth was the expected one, the Messiah.

15. The Scribe travelled for a day and a night before he came across a large group of people who were following a man as he continued on his way from Jericho to Jerusalem.

16. The Scribe approached Jesus and said: *Master, what shall I do to inherit eternal life?*

17. Jesus smiled at the Scribe and said: *What does the letter of the law demand?*

18. The lawyer said: *You shall love the Lord your God with all your heart and your neighbour as yourself.*

19. Jesus said: *Then do so, and you shall live.*

20. *But who is my neighbour?* said the lawyer, thinking he might trap him.

21. Jesus sat down on the side of the dusty road and in answer to the Scribe said: *A merchant, who was travelling on this road, was set upon by a gang of thieves, who robbed him and left him for dead.*

22. *A Pharisee, seeing the man lying in the road, passed by, because he assumed the man was dead, and were he to touch him, he would himself become impure and therefore could never hope to enter the kingdom of heaven.*

23. *Moments later a priest passed by. He also refused to go to the aid of the stricken man, as he feared that if the man was still alive and he touched the flowing blood, he too would become impure and therefore not be able to enter the kingdom of heaven.*

24. *Some time later, a Samaritan passed by and, seeing the body*

lying in the road, immediately went to the merchant's aid. He cleansed and bound the man's wounds, and then lifted him up, placed him on his donkey and accompanied him to the nearest inn. He left the innkeeper with two pence to ensure that the man would be taken care of until he was fully recovered. And before the Samaritan left to continue on his journey, he said, 'And whatever you need to spend, I will repay you when I next pass this way.'

25. Jesus looked up at the Scribe and said: *Which of these men would you say was his neighbour?*

26. The Scribe was annoyed, because it was Jesus who had ended up trapping him into having to admit that it was a Samaritan who turned out to be the man's neighbour.

see
Luke 10:25–37

27. Jesus rose and said: *Then go your way and do likewise.*

28. Jesus continued on his way to Jerusalem, and his disciples followed him.

29. Judas sought out the Scribe, as he could not understand why the Master would tell a parable depicting a Samaritan – the sworn enemies of the Jews – as more likely to show compassion for someone in distress than a Pharisee or a priest.

30. Judas found the lawyer standing at the back of the crowd, seething with anger at his public humiliation in front of such simple people.

31. Judas walked beside him, and began to tell the Scribe of the many good deeds he had witnessed since he had become one of Jesus' followers.

32. The Scribe listened in silence, but it was some time before he calmed down and even began to accept it was possible that Jesus was a holy man.

33. By the time they stopped to rest for the night, Judas hoped

he had convinced the Scribe that he should join them when they entered the Holy City the following day. The Scribe nodded, but remained silent.

34. While they shared supper, Judas' confidence grew. He confided in the lawyer that he too had misgivings about what might happen when his Master set foot in Jerusalem.

35. Judas admitted that he feared that Jesus might be in danger from his many enemies who would be only too happy to see him stumble in his path, even perish.

36. The Scribe suggested: 'Perhaps it might be wise for Jesus not to be seen in Jerusalem at the present time, but instead return to Galilee.'

37. Judas said: 'It is too late for that. The Master has determined his path, and will not countenance turning back. It is the time of the Passover and he believes he is carrying out the will of God.'

38. The Scribe responded: 'Then you must save him from himself, and to that end, you can rely on my help.'

39. Judas listened intently to the Scribe as he suggested how Jesus might be saved.

40. The Scribe even agreed to come to Judas' assistance at any time, should he fear that the Master was in danger.

41. Judas slept soundly for the first time in days, confident that if Jesus faced any danger when he entered Jerusalem, he had enlisted an ally to assist him who was in a position of authority.

42. When Judas rose the following morning, he was told that the lawyer had woken earlier and already set out on the road for Jerusalem.

43. Judas went in search of Jesus and found him walking among his followers. The Master was encouraging them as they prepared for

the final stretch of the journey that would take them to the Holy City.

44. Although the other disciples, even Peter, appeared to be uncertain of what might happen to them, Judas was now confident that when they reached Jerusalem, Jesus would no longer be in any danger.

JUDAS

CHAPTER 17

The Lord hath need of him

1. First they heard the horns, followed by the clamour of voices that grew louder and louder.

2. Citizens were pouring out of the city gates and running up the hill to greet Jesus, as rumour spread that the great teacher was on his way from Bethany.

3. As the crowds grew larger, *Jesus commanded two of his disciples to go into a nearby village. There they would find a donkey that had never been ridden, tethered to a barn door.*

4. Jesus said: *Unleash the animal and bring him to me. Should anyone ask with what authority you do this, you will say, the Lord has need of him, and they will release the beast.*

5. The disciples left Jesus and entered the village, where they found a donkey tied to a barn door. When they released him, someone watching said: *Why are you unleashing the donkey?*

6. The disciples said: *The Lord has need of him*, and the man did not question them again.

7. *They brought the donkey to Jesus, and after a garment had been placed upon its back, Jesus sat upon the beast and continued his journey into Jerusalem*

8. *Many removed their cloaks and spread them in front of Jesus, while others cut down branches from the trees and laid them in his path.*

9. As Jesus approached the city gates, the citizens began waving

palms and cried out: *Hosanna! Blessed is he who comes in the name of the Lord! Blessed is the kingdom of our Father David that is coming! Hosanna in the highest!*

John 12:13

see
Matt 21:2–10;
Mark 11:2–10;
Luke 19:30–36
[xxix]

10. Judas watched in dismay as Jesus passed through the gates and entered the Holy City on a donkey.

11. How could the Master hope to take control of the Temple, and drive out the Romans, astride a donkey, with only an undisciplined group of enthusiastic followers for his army?

12. Judas stared up at the bleak Antonia fortress that overlooked the city, aware that a legion of infantry was billeted inside.

13. At the slightest sign of trouble, the great wooden gates would swing open and a phalanx of Roman soldiers would appear.

14. But the Romans did not even bother to leave their fortress as Jesus made his slow progress towards the Temple, and the crowds, no longer believing that he could possibly be the Messiah, began to dwindle and drift away.

15. Judas had been heartened when blind Bartimaeus had called out to Jesus, *Son of David,* and the Master had not denied him. But Jesus' decision to enter Jerusalem on a donkey would not convince even the simple-minded that this was the Messiah who had come in triumph to finally remove the pagans from the Holy City.

16. Judas shared his misgivings with Peter, who simply reminded

see
Mark 8:33;
Matt 16:23

him of Jesus' words: *Get behind me, Satan; this is the Lord's way, not the way of man, and we must follow God's will.*

17. Judas said: 'But where in our ancient tradition and teaching does it record that the Messiah will enter the Holy City on a donkey?'

18. Peter raised his eyes to heaven and, as if inspired, uttered the words of the Prophet Zechariah:

Rejoice, rejoice, people of Zion!

Shout for joy, you people of Jerusalem!

Look, your king is coming to you!

He comes triumphant and victorious,

but humble and riding on a donkey.

Zech 9:9

19. When Jesus dismounted the donkey, he entered the Temple and prayed.

[xxx]

20. *As it was the evening, he returned to Bethany with some of his disciples to spend the night with Lazarus and his two sisters, Martha and Mary.*

see
John 11:1–4;
Matt 21:17

21. Judas did not accompany his Master to Bethany, but remained in the Temple, where he sought out the Scribe who had befriended him on the road from Jericho.

22. And when Judas found him, he went to the Scribe's home, broke bread, and they shared wine together.

23. And the Scribe said: 'What will he do tomorrow?'

24. Judas answered: 'As it is the Passover, he will return to Jerusalem and go to the Temple. He may perform miracles and cast out demons, and many will believe that he is the Messiah, and for this they will follow him.'

25. The Scribe responded: *Your Master is a good and holy man, but if he allows his followers to indulge in false hopes, it will only end in bloodshed, and the Romans will surely destroy the whole nation.*

see
John 11:48

26. Judas knew that the Scribe spoke the truth and, fearing for his Master's safety, decided to put his trust in this powerful interpreter of the law.

27. Judas confessed: 'I no longer believe that Jesus is the Messiah, but John the Baptist proclaimed that he was a man of God, and therefore we must not let him die at the hands of the Romans.'

see
John 1:32–34,
Mark 1:11

28. The Scribe agreed, and promised to assist Judas with his plans. 'You must spirit Jesus out of the city and, along with the other disciples, accompany him back to Galilee, where the Romans will not trouble him.'

see
Mark 14:10;
Matt 26:15;
Luke 22:6

29. Judas agreed, and before he left, promised the Scribe that *when the time and place were right, he would inform him.*

30. Judas left the home of the Scribe to return to Bethany.

31. As he passed the Antonia fortress, he could hear the Roman soldiers shouting 'Ioudaei sunt porci!', an insult that they were well aware was offensive to all Jews, especially at the time of the Passover.

32. As he left the city and made his way back up the hill to Bethany, Judas felt a great yoke had been lifted from his shoulders, because he alone among the disciples could now save his Master, and with him the fate of Israel.

JUDAS

CHAPTER 18

He must die to save our nation

1. The celebration of the Passover was at hand, and many Jews had travelled from all the regions of Israel, some far beyond, so that they could be in the Holy City to celebrate the feast.

2. Jesus instructed two of his disciples to return to Jerusalem. He said: *Go into the city and you will find a man carrying a pitcher of water. Follow him, and wherever he goes, say to the owner of that home, my Master says, 'Where is the guest chamber? For there I shall eat the Passover with my disciples.' He will show you a large room, furnished and prepared, and you will make ready.*

see Mark 14:12-15; Matt 26:18; Luke 22:8-12

3. A woman entered the home of Martha and Mary in Bethany, where Jesus was resting.

4. *She fell at the feet of Jesus, but did not speak as she broke an alabaster jar open and poured its precious ointment over his feet. She then unbraided her hair and wiped Jesus' feet with it. The whole house was filled with the sweet odour.*

see John 12:3-4

5. Judas grew angry, and could not hide his displeasure. Why had this woman been allowed to touch the body of Jesus, thus flouting the finest traditions of Israel?

6. Judas demanded of the Master: *Why not sell this ointment for three hundred denarii?*

John 12:5

7. Jesus responded: *She did good work, as she performed this act for my burial, and it will be a memorial for her.*

see Mark 14:9; Matt 26:10-13

8. The woman quickly left, but Judas remained racked with doubt.

9. *One or two of the disciples even murmured that Judas wanted to keep the money for himself.*

see
John 12:6

10. Judas remonstrated with Peter, saying: 'The common purse holds barely enough for us to survive.'

11. Peter was unsure of Judas' motives and walked away from him.

12. The Scribe attended the Sanhedrin and informed the Chief Priest of all that Judas had told him.

[xxxi]

13. A Pharisee said: 'What shall we do if Jesus performs many miracles, because then we cannot be seen to oppose him?'

14. Caiaphas, who was the Chief Priest that year, said: *He must die, but not on a feast day, as it will cause uproar among the people.*

see
John 11:48,
Matt 26:1–5,
Mark 14:1–2,
Luke 22:1

15. The Scribe said: *But if we let him alone, our nation could be destroyed.*

16. Caiaphas said: *You do not understand. He must die to save our nation.*

see
John 11:51

17. Another asked: 'How will that come about?'

18. The Scribe answered: 'Judas will lead us to him and we will then arrest Jesus of Nazareth and bring charges against him of being a sinner and a blasphemer.'

19. And then the Scribe said: 'We must let it be known in the Temple that it was one of his disciples who betrayed him.'

John 11:53

20. From that day, the Sanhedrin made plans to put Jesus to death.

JUDAS

CHAPTER 19

Render unto Caesar the things that are Caesar's

1. Jesus came down from Bethany and set out on his journey to the Temple.

2. Vast crowds gathered along the way as Jesus made his slow progress into Jerusalem. By the time he reached the Temple, it was packed with worshippers who had come to hear the great teacher's words and learn from his interpretation of the law.

3. On the path from Bethany, Jesus had been calm and compassionate with all those who flocked around him, but his mood changed the moment he reached the entrance to the Temple.

4. The gentiles had set up a market in the courtyard, with stalls from which the Jews could buy small animals and birds that they would later offer as sacrifices in the Temple.

5. Jesus was unable to hide his anger.

6. He immediately began to turn over the tables where the money dealers exchanged any Roman coins for those of Tyre that bore no human image.

7. Jesus then made a heavy rope of twined cords, and began to drive out the animals from the Temple and release the doves and pigeons from their cages, saying: *Take these things away; you shall not make my Father's house a house of trade.*

8. Judas did not approve of Jesus' disruption of the daily worship because he knew that devout Jews could only carry out ritual

[xxxii]

John 2:16

67

practices in the Temple if trading was allowed in the courtyard.

9. Then one of the Elders asked Jesus: *With what authority do you create this chaos?*

10. Jesus answered: *Destroy the Temple and in three days I shall raise it up.*

11. The Elders responded: *But it has taken forty-six years to build. How can you hope to raise it again in three days?*

John 2:18–20

12. Judas realized that the Master was referring to the promise that after his death, he would rise again in three days; something that he was still unable to accept.

13. Judas stared at the man he loved, and reflected on John the Baptist's words: *Are you he who is to come, or shall we look for another?*

Matt 11:3; Luke 7:19

14. A Sadducee, who could never accept the resurrection as it was against his most cherished beliefs, pressed Jesus to explain what he had meant by this allusion.

15. Jesus answered: *The God of Abraham, Isaac and Jacob is God of the living. Therefore these great patriarchs must still be alive in the resurrection.*

see Mark 12:24–27; Matt 22:31–32; Luke 20:37–38

16. Another Elder stepped forward, also hoping to get the better of Jesus, and asked: *Great teacher, we know that you are truthful, even to the point of not caring what others may think of you, or whom you might offend, so tell us, is it against the law to pay taxes to a Roman Emperor?*

17. Jesus said, *Bring me a coin.* The same man handed him a coin that bore the imprint of Caesar. Jesus said: *Whose image is on this coin?*

18. *Caesar's,* answered the Elder.

see Mark 12:13–17; Matt 22:15–22; Luke 20:20–26

19. Jesus mocked him and said: *Render unto Caesar the things that are Caesar's, and render unto God the things that are God's.*

20. Then a Scribe stepped forward.

21. Judas immediately recognized him as the man who had promised to assist if Jesus were in any danger.

22. The Scribe asked a question that went to the very heart of Jewish tradition: *Is the Messiah the Son of David?*

23. Jesus responded with the words of David, as recorded in the hymns of Israel: *The Lord said to my Lord, 'Sit at my right hand, till I make your enemies my footstool.'*

see Psalm 110:1

24. Jesus then turned his attention to the crowd that surrounded him and declared *If David calls the Messiah 'my Lord', then the Messiah cannot be David's son.*

see Mark 12:35–37; Matt 22:41–46; Luke 20:40–41

25. While those around him were overwhelmed by his teaching and interpretation of the law, several of the Elders and the Pharisees immediately left the Temple to sit in the council of the Sanhedrin.

26. When they met, they confirmed that Jesus must die.

JUDAS

CHAPTER 20

One of you here present will betray me

1. Jesus and his disciples met together in the upper room to which Peter and Andrew had been led so they might celebrate the Passover feast.

2. When they sat down for supper, the disciples began to whisper among themselves.

3. They were anxious after what had taken place at the Temple that morning, and even feared that the Master's mood might suddenly change once again.

4. They admitted one to the other that they no longer knew what would come to pass, either for Jesus or themselves.

see
Mark 14:17–21;
Matt 26:20–25;
Luke 22:14, 21–23

5. When Jesus eventually raised his hands and spoke, they were all taken by surprise by his words: *One of you here present, who eats with me tonight, will betray me.*

6. Each of them in turn insisted that it could not be him.

7. Judas knew that he was innocent of such an accusation, as his only purpose was to save Jesus from an unnecessary death.

8. Peter was the most vehement in his denial. He protested that it could not be him, for he would be willing to lay down his life for Jesus before he would betray him.

Mark 14:30;
Matt 26:34;
Luke 22:34

9. Jesus looked at Peter sadly and said: *I tell you that even this night, before the cock crows twice, you will deny me three times.*

10. Peter responded with even more passion: *I would die with you*

before that could take place.

11. Jesus closed his eyes and began to perform the ceremony of the Passover, marked by the symbolic raising of bitter herbs, bread, wine and other symbols, to relive the story of how the Exodus unfolds.

12. The disciples recognized that this re-enactment of the Exodus was no mere gesture, as all Jews believe that God is present at the Passover table.

13. However, when Jesus opened his eyes and raised the unleavened bread, he did not, as the disciples expected, refer to the gift of manna given during the Exodus.

14. When he spoke, they were greeted with unfamiliar words: *Take, eat, this is my body, given for you, do this in remembrance of me.*

15. Each disciple took of the bread and ate it.

16. Jesus then raised the cup of wine without mentioning the historic moment when God parted the Red Sea, but instead proclaimed: *This is my blood, which is shed for many. Do this in remembrance of me.*

17. The disciples, in turn, drank the wine, even though they feared Jesus was referring to his imminent death.

18. Judas still believed that not only could he save the Master, but his fellow disciples would rejoice at his bold initiative.

19. *After receiving the morsel of bread, Judas immediately went out and it was night.*

20. He made his way quickly to the home of the Scribe, who welcomed him.

21. The Scribe told Judas: 'I have gathered together many loyal supporters of Jesus, whose single purpose is to save him from an unnecessary death.'

22. Judas thanked him, and said to the Scribe: 'After the Passover

see
Mark 14:31;
Matt 26:35

[xxxiii]

see
Cor I 11:24–25;
Mark 14:22–24;
Matt 26:26–28;
Luke 22:20

John 13:30

feast, Jesus will go to the Mount of Olives, where he and the other disciples may be found at prayer.

23. 'When you come, I will identify the Master, so that together, we can return to Galilee, and save him from an unnecessary death.'

JUDAS

CHAPTER 21

Master, Master

1. Judas left the Scribe's home and made his way to the Mount of Olives.

2. When he came to a place called Gethsemane, he found Jesus on his knees, deep in prayer.

3. *Many of Jesus' followers were scattered around the mountain, some praying, while others were fast asleep.*

4. Judas approached the Master and, when he was a few paces off, fell on his knees and joined him in prayer.

5. Jesus rose suddenly and, raising his arms towards the heavens, said: *Abba, with you, all things are possible; take away this cup from me; however, not what I will, but what you command.*

6. When Judas heard these words, he was filled with hope that the Master might agree to return to Galilee and avoid the death he had earlier foretold.

7. Judas walked slowly towards Jesus. He threw his arms round his neck and said: *'Master, Master,' and kissed him.*

8. Jesus took him in his arms, and Judas was overcome with his compassion.

9. Suddenly, out of the darkness appeared a band of officers from the Temple, who were carrying lanterns, torches, cudgels, sticks and other weapons.

10. Jesus released Judas and turned towards them, *for he knew all*

see
John 18:2;
Mark 14:26;
Matt 26:30;
Luke 22:39

see
Mark 14:36;
Matt 26:39;
Luke 22:42

Mark 14:45;
Matt 26:49;
Luke 22:47–48

John 18:4

things that would happen to him.

11. Judas reeled back in horror, suddenly aware that the Master had been referring to him when he had said during the Passover feast:

see
Mark 14:18

One of you will betray me, even one of the twelve.

12. *Jesus then turned to the officers and asked: 'Whom do you seek?'*

13. *They answered: 'Jesus of Nazareth.'*

John 18:4–5

14. *Jesus said to them: 'I am he.'*

15. Judas was shocked to see that among the group who had come to arrest Jesus was the Scribe who had claimed to be his friend.

16. Judas charged angrily towards him, his fists flying in every direction as he cried out: 'You have betrayed me.' But two of the officers grabbed him by the arms and held him back. Judas spat on him.

17. Jesus looked at the Scribe, and said: *Am I to be treated as a thief, that you come in the night armed with swords and staves to arrest me? Day after day I attended you in the Temple and you did not approach*

see
Mark 14:48–49;
Matt 26:55;
Luke 22:52–53

me, but you have now chosen this moment in the darkest hour of the night to arrest me.

18. As the guards continued to hold on to Judas, the Scribe turned to Jesus and said: *You do not understand. It is better that one should die*

see
John 11:50

for the people than the whole nation should be destroyed.

19. The disciples were suddenly woken from their slumbers and, seeing Jesus surrounded by soldiers and officers of the Temple, were filled with fear.

see
Mark 14:50

20. *They all forsook Jesus and ran away.*

21. *Even as they fled, a soldier grabbed one of Jesus' followers, who was wearing only a loin cloth round his body, but the young man shed*

see
Mark 14:51–52

the garment and escaped naked.

22. The officers then released Judas, who stood his ground and watched as Jesus was led away.

JUDAS

CHAPTER 22

I do not know the man

1. Judas waited until the group of officers that surrounded his Master was out of sight before he followed in their footsteps, always keeping his distance.

2. Although Judas no longer believed that Jesus was the Messiah, he had never lost faith in John the Baptist's judgment: *He is a man of God.*

see
John 1:34

3. Judas hoped that even at this late hour there might be some way of rescuing Jesus.

4. He watched as Jesus was escorted to the house of Caiaphas, the Chief Priest, where a trial would take place, and a verdict would be handed down that had already been agreed upon.

5. Judas pulled the top of his robe over his head and disappeared into the shadows behind a pillar in the courtyard.

6. He listened to the gullible and innocent as they talked among themselves, passing on the latest rumour that was being circulated by well-placed Scribes and officers of the Sanhedrin.

7. One said: 'Jesus of Nazareth has been arrested and charged with blasphemy.'

8. Another: 'No one was willing to come forward in his defence.'

9. And yet another: 'All his disciples ran away the moment they saw the officers of the Temple.'

10. Judas stepped out of the shadows. Even at this last moment he

hoped that the Scribe would confirm his story, and the Sanhedrin would allow Jesus to return to Galilee, as long as he gave them an assurance that he would never again be seen in Jerusalem.

11. And then he saw a stooped figure on the far side of the courtyard.

12. Judas approached Peter, confident that together they could bear witness for Jesus, and perhaps even at this late hour save his life.

13. A serving girl stopped and, looking at Peter, said: *I saw you with Jesus of Galilee.*

14. Peter said: *I do not know the man.*

15. And another attendant turning to look at Peter, said: *This man was a follower of Jesus,* and once again, Peter denied ever knowing him.

16. A cock crowed once.

17. A little later, others came up to Peter and said: *You were with Jesus of Nazareth,* and he denied him a third time.

18. Judas heard the cock crow a second time.

19. And then Peter recalled Jesus' words: *Before the cock crows twice, you will deny me three times.*

20. Judas followed Peter as he stole out of the courtyard to hide among the milling crowd. *His head was bowed, and he was weeping bitterly.*

21. Although both of them had failed their Master in his hour of need, Judas still believed they could be redeemed.

22. Peter turned to discover who was following him, and when he saw it was Judas, he shouted: *It would be better for you not to have been born.*

23. Judas felt betrayed. He had not run away when the Master was arrested.

24. He had not, like Peter, denied Jesus three times, just as the

see
Matt 26:69–75;
Mark 14:66–72;
Luke 22:56–62

Mark 14:21;
Matt 26:24

Master had foretold. Why was he the only one to be branded as a sinner?

25. Judas returned to the courtyard and waited hour upon hour for the Master to reappear.

26. Priests continued to enter and leave the home of Caiaphas so that the latest scraps of information could be passed on to willing ears that only wanted to hear bad news.

27. *Jesus of Nazareth is claiming that he is the Son of God.*

28. *The Sanhedrin has found him guilty of blasphemy. He is a sinner.*

see
Mark 14:62–64;
Matt 26:65–66;
Luke 22:70–71

29. The word quickly spread that Jesus had been betrayed by one of his own disciples.

30. 'Name him,' shouted a well-placed onlooker.

31. The Scribe immediately stepped forward. 'Judas Iscariot,' he declared so that all might know his name.

32. Judas bowed his head as the crowd began to chant: 'Betrayer, betrayer, betrayer.'

33. Judas turned to the Scribe and pleaded with him to confess what had actually taken place.

34. The Scribe smiled and, pointing to Judas, declared: 'Behold the betrayer.'

35. Judas wept.

JUDAS

CHAPTER 23

My God, my God, why have you forsaken me?

1. Jesus emerged from the house of Caiaphas bound but unbowed, his face covered in spittle.

2. He was led away to the Governor's fortress, where the Chief Priest handed their prisoner over to Pontius Pilate.

3. The Scribes and the Pharisees did not want to be seen passing judgment, as they had no desire to have Jesus' death laid at their door.

4. If anything were to go wrong, they would insist that it was the Romans who had made the final decision.

5. A large and boisterous crowd was assembling at the fortress gates. They were being whipped up into a frenzy as they waited for Pilate's judgment.

Mark 15:14;
Matt 27:22;
Luke 23:21;
John 19:6

6. The Scribes and the Pharisees mingled among the crowd, coaxing them to demand: *Crucify him, crucify him.*

7. Judas remained powerless as he searched among the crowd for a familiar face, hoping to find a disciple who would join him, and counter, 'Save him, save him.' But his was a lone voice, overwhelmed by the brutal cries of the masses.

8. The roar grew louder as Pilate led Jesus out on to the balcony.

see
John 19:5

9. *Jesus was clothed in a purple robe and wearing a crown of thorns.*

see
Luke 23:4
[xxxiv]

10. *Pilate said: Behold the King of the Jews in whom I can find no fault.*

11. The crowd responded with raucous chants of: *Crucify him,*

crucify him, and so loud became the clamour that Pilate retreated into the safety of the Antonia fortress.

12. The crowd fell silent as they listened to the lashes being administered by Pilate's guards, and when Jesus appeared a second time, he was wearing only a loin cloth and his body was cut and bleeding.

see
Luke 23:22;
Mark 15:14;
Matt 27:23;
John 19:4

13. Pilate said: *I bring him to you, but I find no fault in him.*

14. But the cries of *Crucify him, crucify him,* only grew louder, causing Pilate to retreat once again, fearful that he might be the cause of an uprising among the people.

15. When Pilate appeared a third time, Jesus stood on one side of him, while a murderer called Barabbas, who had been brought up from the dungeons, stood on the other.

16. It being the Passover and that time of the year, Pilate offered the crowd the chance to save one of the condemned men from execution.

17. *Barabbas, Barabbas,* they cried in unison.

18. Pilate said: *Shall I crucify your King?*

19. The Chief Priest responded: *We have no King but Caesar.*

20. Pilate said: *Then take him away, and may his blood be upon you.*

see
Mark 15:6-15;
Matt 27:15–26;
Luke 23:18–25;
John 18:39–40;
19:15

21. Judas watched as Pilate scurried back into the confines of the fortress, where he found his wife weeping.

22. Having surrendered his authority to the baying crowd, *Pilate washed his hands.*

see
Matt 27:24

23. As Jesus was led away, Judas searched around the packed square, still hoping to find one or two of his fellow disciples. He found none.

24. His eyes settled on a group of women.

25. Judas bowed his head in shame, when he recognized *Mary Magdalene, Mary the mother of James and Joseph, and the other women who had travelled with them from Galilee.*

see
Luke 8:1–3; 23:55;
Mark 15:40–41;
Matt 27:55–56

26. *They had not forsaken Jesus, but had remained constant.*

see
Luke 23:28

27. The women wept when Jesus appeared in the square.

28. *He was surrounded by soldiers who were there to make sure that* John 19:17 *he carried his own cross to the place of execution.*

29. As Jesus dragged the heavy cross through the crowded streets, see Mark 15:26–30; Matt 27:37–40 passers-by spat on him, while others mocked: *Is this the King of the Jews who has come to rule over us?*

30. Judas recalled the many occasions when Jesus had warned the disciples against ever calling him *the King of the Jews*.

see Mark 15:36; Matt 27:34; John 19:29
31. *A soldier, aware that the prisoner was gasping for breath, filled a sponge with vinegar and cruelly pressed it to his mouth, but Jesus rejected it.*

Mark 15:21; Matt 27:32; Luke 23:26
32. *After a few more steps, Jesus collapsed on the ground and one of the guards forced a man called Simon, who had come from Cyrenia to visit the city, to carry his cross.*

33. The women remained by his side as Jesus continued on his slow, humiliating progress to a site named Golgotha — *meaning the place of the skull* — where they nailed him to a cross.

34. But before the cross could be raised in its place, a soldier, Mark 15:26; Matt 27:37; John 19:19 carrying out the orders of Pilate, attached the superscription: *The King of the Jews.*

35. At the same time, two other crosses were raised on either side of him, and Judas recalled that the scripture had foretold: *And he was* see Isaiah 53:12 *numbered with the transgressors.*

36. One of the prisoners hanging by his side shouted: *If you are the Messiah, save yourself and us at the same time.*

37. But the other prisoner remonstrated with him and said: *We are guilty of our offences, while he did nothing wrong,* and turning to Jesus, pleaded: *Remember me when you return as King.*

Luke 23:39–43
38. Jesus said to him: *Today you will be with me in paradise.*

39. Judas watched as the soldiers stationed at the foot of the cross

played dice, before they divided Jesus' garments into four parts so that the promise of David's song might be fulfilled.

see
Psalm 22:18

40. Jesus said: *Father, forgive them, for they know not what they do.*

41. Judas watched as the Elders and the Scribes continued to torment Jesus: *He saved others, now let him save himself.*

42. They said: *Let us see the Messiah come down from the cross that we might believe in him.*

43. Another said: *Are you not the same man who was going to tear down the Temple and then build it up again in three days?*

44. *And darkness fell upon the earth, and the curtain that hung in the Temple was torn from top to bottom.*

45. Judas fell on his knees. He prayed that the Master might be spared any more suffering and allowed to die quickly.

46. But it was not until the ninth hour that Jesus cried out: *My God, my God, why have you forsaken me?*

47. A centurion, who was stationed at the foot of the cross, looked up at Jesus and said: *Truly, this man was the Son of God.*

48. Judas remained on his knees praying, until the cross was finally lowered.

49. *Now there stood by the cross Jesus' loyal women followers.*

50. The soldiers checked to be sure the prisoner was dead before they would allow the women to take away his body.

51. *Once they removed his body from the cross, Mary Magdalene bathed his wounds, while Mary, the mother of James, cleansed his body. They covered him in a white robe and carried him away.*

see
Mark 15:25–47;
Matt 27:35–61;
Luke 23:33–56

52. As Jesus' body was carried away, Judas looked up to the heavens and repeated John the Baptist's words: *Are you he who is to come, or shall we look for another?*

Luke 7:19;
Matt 11:3

53. That was the last time Judas saw the Master.

JUDAS

CHAPTER 24

Cursed is anyone who hangs from a tree

1. The Passover was at hand, and already some Jews were murmuring among themselves that it had been a mistake to condone the killing of a holy man.

2. These were the same people who had willingly chanted the words, *Crucify him, crucify him,* only days before, but were now quickly shifting the blame for the death of Jesus on to Pontius Pilate and his Roman cohorts.

3. The rest of the disciples had gone into hiding, while the name spat out of everyone's lips was that of Judas Iscariot, *the man who had betrayed Jesus.*

see
Matt 26:15

4. Rumours were already spreading through the city, each new one quickly overtaken by another.

see
Mark 16:4–7;
Matt 28:2–7;
Luke 24:2–5

5. It was said that *the rock that had closed Jesus' tomb had been rolled aside and that there had been a vision of angels.*

6. It was even claimed that Jesus had risen from the dead, and had been sighted on three occasions: *by Mary Magdalene — she had seen him outside the tomb on the third day and mistaken him for a gardener; by two of the disciples on the road to Emmaus, and by eleven of the disciples while sharing supper together.*

see
John 20:14–15;
Luke 24;
Mark 16:19–20

7. The Elders and the Pharisees were attempting to ridicule any suggestion that Jesus had risen from the dead.

see
Matt 28:11–15

8. However, they were losing their authority with the people, and

could do nothing about those Jews who were forsaking the faith of their ancestors to join a new sect, which believed that Jesus had risen from the dead.

9. Peter had become the leader of these converts and was claiming *that the spirit of God had been given to this small group in Jerusalem.* *see* Acts 2:2–13

10. Judas could not accept that Jesus had risen from the dead, and he parted company with Peter.

11. He held on to John the Baptist's belief that Jesus was a holy man, even a prophet, who followed in the tradition of Jeremiah, Isaiah and Ezekiel.

12. But Judas no longer accepted that Jesus was the chosen one, destined to rescue the Jews from their oppressors.

13. Judas continued to believe that YHWH was their god, and Israel the chosen people.

14. Had not Moses prophesied, *Cursed is anyone who hangs from a tree?* Deut 21:23

15. Because of all that had taken place, Judas was now a marked man, with no friends to protect him.

16. Whenever he showed his face in the Synagogue, the Elders rejected him, as they did not wish to be reminded who had led them to Jesus.

17. Shunned by the Jewish leaders and abandoned by the followers of Jesus, after thirty days Judas departed from the Holy City and set out on the long journey to Khirbet Qumran.

18. There he joined the community of Essenes, who lived in a fortress on the shores of the Salt Sea and were committed to spending the rest of their days in the solitude of the desert.

19. Although the Essenes detested the Romans, they despised the Sadducees with equal passion.

20. They considered the Sadducees had forfeited their moral authority to be the chosen leaders of Israel by colluding with the pagans to ensure that they remained in office and retained their vested privileges.

21. The Essenes also disapproved of the Pharisees, who they believed were no longer interpreting the fine traditions of Israel.

22. In contrast, the Essenes devoted their lives to re-enacting the desert experience of the Exodus of the Jews from Egypt.

23. They awaited the coming of the Messiah, who would surely vanquish all God's enemies before ascending the throne on that great and terrible day when the kingdom of Israel would be restored to the Jewish people.

24. Although Judas devoted the rest of his life to working with the Essenes, not a day passed when he did not fall on his knees and mourn the death of Jesus.

JUDAS

CHAPTER 25

The sins of the father

1. I had not seen my father since I was a child of eight years, when he left for Jerusalem as a trusted disciple of Jesus of Nazareth.

2. I would never have discovered his fate had not a wandering preacher who was passing through Kerioth told me that he had come across my father while visiting Khirbet Qumran.

3. Within days, and with the blessing of my family, I left to make the long journey across the Judean desert to the Salt Sea, so that I might be reunited with my father.

4. The Essenes reluctantly allowed me to enter their gates, but not before I had been able to convince them that I was the first born of Judas Iscariot.

5. When I first saw my father I did not recognize him, for he had grown old and did not know me.

6. Once Abba had accepted that I was his son, he warned me that I could only stay for a month and a day, unless I was willing to enrol with the Essenes, and spend the rest of my life in the solitude of the desert preparing for the coming of the Messiah.

7. It was not until the third day that I asked my father to explain why he had not returned to Kerioth to defend his good name.

8. Abba believed that his very presence would continually remind all around him of the unwitting role he had played in the death of Jesus.

Mark 14:21;
Matt 26:24

9. He could also never forget Peter's parting words: *It would be better for you not to have been born.*

10. Once he had told me of that final encounter with Peter, he made no further reference to his days as a disciple of Jesus of Nazareth.

11. He only seemed interested to talk about our family and what had become of them.

12. I did not answer all the questions Abba put to me, as I had no desire to acquaint him with the fact that even distant relatives were daily reminded that they shared the same blood as Judas Iscariot, the disciple who had betrayed Jesus.

13. I did tell him that my mother had given up her spirit at the age of two score years and three, after two of my brothers had fled from Israel to live in far-off lands.

14. Later, I admitted that none of my sisters was married, and I had yet to produce a son.

15. Abba's only response was that *the sins of the father would surely*

Deut 5:9

be visited on the third and fourth generation.

16. With each new revelation, Abba became more and more desolate.

17. For days, no words passed his lips, and I feared for his life.

18. It was not until the eleventh day that he began to speak again, and then only to acquaint me with his work during those years of self-imposed exile at Khirbet Qumran.

19. He and his fellow Essenes had laboured night and day to build a library of scrolls that would ensure that the history of the Jewish people would not be lost, however long the pagan invaders inhabited the Holy Land.

20. Moreover, the Romans had become more and more authoritarian after their informers had warned them of a possible

uprising among the people.

21. Titus had issued an edict declaring that all establishments that refused to open their gates to the Romans were to be razed to the ground and their inhabitants sentenced to death for defying the authority of Caesar.

22. Legions of Roman forces swept through the land of Israel carrying out the Supreme Commander's orders.

23. Following the sacking of Jerusalem, Judas told me that he feared it would not be long before the Romans crossed the desert and turned their attention to Khirbet Qumran.

24. Whenever my father spoke, it was only to talk of our ancient past, and I was beginning to despair that he would ever refer to those days when he had been a disciple of Jesus of Nazareth.

25. That changed when he asked if I had any knowledge of what had become of the other eleven disciples.

26. I told him of a document that had been circulating among the Christians in Antioch and another that had appeared more recently in Ephesus.

27. My father listened to these revelations in disbelief.

28. Judas poured scorn on the writer who claimed that he had seen Jesus walk on water, and another who suggested that while at a wedding feast in Cana he had watched the Master turn water into wine. These things never happened he declared.

29. While he pondered these affairs I remained silent.

30. It was not until he pressed me again that I reluctantly admitted that another gospel was being spread abroad reporting that Peter had given a direction to say that Judas' name should be struck from the list of those disciples who had originally been chosen by Jesus.

[xxxvi]

see Josephus, Jewish War VI.323–355 [xxxvii]

see Matt 14:22–27; John 2:1–10 [xxxviii]

see
Acts 1:21–26
[xxxix]

31. *He was to be replaced by one Matthias, who had been selected by lot, and would in future be numbered as one of the twelve apostles.*

32. 'Why, why?' he demanded to know.

see
Matt 27:5

33. 'Because one of the apostles recorded that Judas had hanged himself.'

34. Judas responded immediately: 'If only he had remembered their traditional upbringing, he would have recalled that no pious Jew would ever consider taking his own life.'

[xl]

35. I warned my father that yet another had written that Judas had fallen and his body had burst asunder.

Acts 1:18

36. Abba pondered on these words before saying: 'If either of these reports were accurate – and clearly they could not both be – surely such an act would have been confirmed by the other apostles, so that all Christians might know how Judas had ended his life.

37. 'And what other blasphemies do these men spread abroad?' he said quietly.

38. I did not reply, although I was unable to hide my distress.

39. 'Tell me everything,' Abba demanded, 'so that I might know what my fellow disciples say of me.'

see
Matt 26:15
[xli]

40. I bowed my head and whispered that one of them had written: 'Judas had betrayed his Master in return for thirty pieces of silver.'

41. When Abba heard these words, he could no longer control his temper.

42. It was then that Judas demanded his own account should be recorded so that all may know the truth of what had taken place during the time he had been a disciple of the Prophet Jesus.

43. I spent my final days at Khirbet Qumran, taking down his every word.

44. Like so many old men, Abba could recall every detail of what

had happened forty years before, while barely remembering what had taken place the previous day.

45. I could have written much more, but when the Essenes learned from a passing stranger that a legion of Roman soldiers had been seen crossing the Judean desert in the direction of Khirbet Qumran, Abba insisted that I should make haste, leave and return home.

46. I wanted to go on setting down my father's words, but his mind was now preoccupied with my safety and the likely consequences of the approaching Roman army.

47. I obeyed Abba's command and, placing the several pages of this manuscript in a leather pouch, reluctantly left him to go back to my family in Kerioth.

48. Many of the Essenes had already deserted the compound and fled south, to take refuge in the fortress at Masada.

[xlii]

49. When they left, I witnessed several of them carrying manuscripts on their persons.

50. I later learned that such was their passion in all things that at Masada the Essenes chose to die by their own hand, rather than be captured, taken back to Rome and paraded in front of the pagans on a victory march.

51. I fear that all the trouble the Essenes had taken over the years to preserve their treasured scrolls must surely have been in vain.

52. Judas was three score years and ten at that time, and too feeble to contemplate the steep climb that would have taken him to the relative safety of Masada.

53. Judas, along with a handful of his companions, remained resolutely inside the compound of Khirbet Qumran.

54. The gates of the fortress were locked and barred as they awaited the approach of the Roman army.

55. Four days later the compound was overrun by a legion of Roman soldiers.

56. Judas was arrested and along with seven of his companions, sentenced to death without trial.

57. Judas fell on his knees when the sentence was pronounced.

58. He gave thanks to YHWH when he learned that he would suffer the same fate as Jesus.

[xliii]

59. Judas died as Jesus did. He was crucified by the Romans.

GLOSSARY

THE GLOSSARY *provides clarifications for certain details of* The Gospel According to Judas, *written against the background of a first-century world.*

HIGHLIGHTED PASSAGES *in* The Gospel According to Judas *are either direct citations from the biblical text, or paraphrases of it. Sources are always indicated, but the citation of the biblical source is preceded by 'see'.*

ALL BIBLICAL TEXTS *are an original translation of the author(s), guided by the Revised StandardVersion and the New Revised StandardVersion.*

i. GOSPELS: The Gospels were written late in the first century (Mark: *circa* AD70, Matthew: *circa* AD85, Luke: *circa* AD85, John: *circa* AD100). We do not know the identity of the Evangelists, as the names Matthew, Mark, Luke and John were all added to manuscripts late in the second century. It is probable that none of the Evangelists was an Apostle. Christian tradition holds that Mark was a close associate of Peter in Rome, but not an Apostle. Matthew was a well-instructed Jew who became a Christian (see Matt 13:52). The fact that the name of the tax collector (Levi) in Mark 2:14 (see also Luke 5:27) becomes 'Matthew' in Matt 9:9 may be a self-identification of the Apostle Matthew (see Matt 10:3; Mark 3:18; Luke 6:15), but this is not proof positive. 'The Beloved Disciple' of the Fourth Gospel was identified as John late in the second century. The author of the Fourth Gospel was more likely an ex-disciple of John the Baptist who became a close follower of Jesus, but not one of the Twelve. The Christian Church regards the four Gospels as 'Sacred Scripture'. They are narrative descriptions of what God did for humankind through the life, teaching, death and resurrection of Jesus.

ii. FATHERS AND SONS: As a result of the empire created by Alexander the Great (336–323BC), Greek was the language commonly spoken and used for written communication throughout the Mediterranean basin, and beyond. All the documents of the New Testament, the product of a Jewish world, are written in Greek. The 'family' (the *bet-'ab*: 'the house of the father') is the most important unit in the nation, and for the survival of the individual. The numerous genealogical lists in both the Old and the New Testament (see, for example, Gen 36:9–14; 1 Chron

9:39–44; Matt 1:1–17; Luke 3:23–38) show how crucial it was to 'own' one's patrimony. As well as economic and social patrimony, sons had a responsibility to continue the traditions of their fathers. This responsibility is powerfully presented in the Jewish document *The Testament of the Twelve Patriarchs*, and also in *Ben Sirach*. In the former the 'sons' are instructed by their father to pass on his tradition, and the latter is a text that shows this being carried out with respect by a grandson. This book, also known as Ecclesiasticus, originally written in Hebrew, was translated into Greek before the Christian era.

iii. GOSPELS NOT ACCEPTED BY THE CHRISTIANS: There were many 'gospels', known as 'apocryphal gospels', that were not accepted by the emerging Church. A collection of such gospel material, written in Coptic, but originally in Greek, *The Codex Tchacos*, was made public in 1999. Several fragments of a 'Gospel of Judas' can be found in the codex, and these possibly date back to AD180. The text is fragmentary, not really a 'gospel', and is representative of a second-century Gnostic understanding of Jesus. Judas is presented as someone who is encouraged by Jesus to do God's will by setting in motion the action that will liberate Jesus from the wicked human condition to become a heavenly figure. For a discussion by the Archbishop of Durham, see T. Wright, *Judas and the Gospel of Jesus* (London: SPCK, 2006). *The Gospel According to Judas* recorded here was not inspired by this text, but attempts to present the Christian story through the eyes of Judas.

iv. THE NAME 'JUDAS ISCARIOT': As well as the explanation of the surname Iscariot put forward in *The Gospel According To Judas* 1:12–15, several other hypotheses have been advanced, e.g. that Judas was a 'deliverer' on the basis of the Hebrew root verb, *skr*. The name 'Judas' is a Greek form of the Hebrew 'Judah'.

v. THE BIRTH OF JESUS: Judas' understanding of the birth of Jesus is not the 'Roman Catholic' interpretation, as expressed in the Marian doctrines, especially that of Mary's perpetual virginity. It is, however, a widely accepted understanding of such texts as Matthew 1:25; Mark 3:31–35; 6:3; John 7:3–8. Judas, like any strictly brought-up Jew, could only accept Jesus as the first born of a lawful Jewish wedlock.

vi. SEXUAL UNIONS BETWEEN ANGELS AND WOMEN: Pre-Christian and Rabbinic traditions look back on the unions between angels and human women, as told in Genesis 6:1–4, as the source of evil and the presence of giants in the world. So serious was this evil that God regretted putting Adam and Eve on the earth. His heart grieved, and in the destruction that followed, only Noah and his family survived (see Gen 6:1–9:17). See the development of Gen 6:1–4 in the Qumran documents (e.g. 4QBook of Giants) and in 1 Enoch (see 1 Enoch 6 and 7).

vii. TOUCHING A WOMAN: Jesus' touching a woman who is not his wife would be regarded as a breach of piety. Later Rabbinic legislation prohibits a woman from serving at table, as the private matter of a woman's menstrual cycle could not be ascertained. For the biblical background of this custom, see Lev 15:19–24; 18:6; 22:10; 36:17, and the tractate *Niddah* in the Mishnah. As Rabbi Samuel (died *circa* AD254) said: 'One must under no circumstance be served by a woman, be she adult or child.'

viii. THE DAVIDIC THRONE: King David was Israel's second and greatest king. He ruled from about 1010–970BC, and built an empire that stretched from Egypt into present-day Iran. Psalm 89:4 and 2 Sam 23:5 speak explicitly of an everlasting covenant between YHWH and David. There are many understandings of how this promise was to be fulfilled. One of them is that YHWH will raise up a 'Son of David' who would be restored to a royal throne in Jerusalem. He would once again establish the glory of Israel by means of great military victories. Christians believe that Jesus does fulfil the promises of the Davidic covenant (see Matt 1:1; Rom 1:3), but Jesus never accepted the role of a potential military leader. The Gospels suggest that the first disciples may have followed him in the hope that he would.

ix. THE SCRIBES AND THE PHARISEES: The Scribes were largely a servant group. They were men who studied the law and served as legal consultants to anyone who required their expert services. Thus, there were Scribes of the Sadducees and well as Scribes of the Pharisees. The Pharisees emerged in Israel during the two centuries before the Christian era. At that time Jewish leadership, including the High Priest, was controlled by foreign powers, initially the Hellenistic leaders, and then the Romans. The Pharisees (whose name probably reflects the concept of being 'cut off' from corruption) attempted to live a strict Jewish life, obedient to the commands of the Torah. They opposed corrupt leadership and suffered a great deal because of their faith. They travelled wherever there were Jews, but their base was always the Synagogue, where the Torah was the centre of Jewish worship. Their focus on the Torah and Synagogue ensured mobility; thus they survived the Jewish War and eventually produced what is known as Rabbinic Judaism.

x. UNDER A FIG TREE: There is a Jewish tradition that a person reflecting on the Torah should do so under a fig tree. The Jewish texts are late, but probably refer to a widespread and early tradition of the learned men of the law sitting under a fig tree to study scripture.

xi. THE SON OF GOD: Judas does not believe that Jesus is the 'Son of God', as is found in the Johannine tradition (AD100), and as it was eventually understood and defined by the Church at Nicea (AD325) and Chalcedon (AD451): Jesus as the second person in the Trinity. Judas does believe in the messianic 'son of God', as expected in Israel on the basis of such texts as Ps 2:7 and 2 Sam 7:14.

xii. SIN AND SICKNESS: The Hebrew Bible often links the punishment of sin with sickness and death (2 Sam 12:13–23; 24:1–25). Only God has authority over sickness and sin.

xiii. CONFLICT STORIES: The description of the conflicts between Jesus and the Jewish leadership, found in *The Gospel According to Judas* 6:9–15, is based on Mark 2:1–12. Judas' account suggests a mounting crisis. The initial response to Jesus' miracles is surprise. By the time he has performed all of his miracles, the Jewish Elders have judged him to be a blasphemer, and only worthy of death.

xiv. THE DECAPOLIS: This term refers to a group of Hellenistic towns located in Transjordania, the region to the north-east of the river Jordan. The word in Greek means 'ten cities', but it is difficult to trace the exact names of ten cities. The following nine have been identified: Abila, Canata, Dius, Gadara, Gerasa, Hippos, Pella, Phildelphia and Scythopolis. These cities were largely inhabited by Gentiles, who followed Greek customs and religion.

xv. THE TWELVE: The list of the twelve disciples in *The Gospel According to Judas* 8:30 reflects the lists in the Christian Gospels. Judas Iscariot is always named last. The placing of Judas' name at the end of the list and his delineation as the one who betrayed Jesus were all part of the early Christian determination to blacken Judas' character.

xvi. JESUS' SERMON: The sermon of Jesus, beginning with the 'beatitudes', is loosely based on Jesus' sermon on the plain as found in Luke (6:20–49), rather than the longer, better-known version of the Sermon on the Mount (Matt 5, 6 and 7).

xvii. OUR FATHER. The version of the 'Our Father' found in *The Gospel According to Judas* 9:37 is based on the Lucan version of this prayer (Luke 11:2–4). It is very brief, and full of urgent promises that look to an imminent fulfilment. The version in the Gospel of Luke is likely to be closer to the words that Jesus actually taught the disciples than the elaborate and better-known form of the prayer, found in Matt 6:9–13, which is currently used in most Christian liturgies and prayer books.

xviii. THE COMMUNITY AT KHIRBET QUMRAN: The discovery of the Dead Sea Scrolls (*circa* 1947) led to the uncovering of a fortress-like building at Khirbet Qumran, close to the Dead Sea, which housed a community of pious Jews. The building stood from about 150BC until AD70, when it was destroyed by the Romans. It is widely accepted that a group of Jewish sectarians, known by other first-century witnesses as the Essenes, had gathered at Khirbet Qumran. They lived in community, and were hostile to a Jewish leadership that compromised the traditions of Israel in order to maintain good relations with foreign powers. Since 1947, many scrolls, some containing biblical texts and others containing texts that had been composed at Qumran, have been unearthed. The texts mentioned (*Community Rule*, *Rule of the Congregation*, *The War Scroll*) were written by the Essenes at Khirbet Qumran.

xix. THE MESSIAH AND THE BREAD FROM HEAVEN: The link between the gift of the manna and the messianic era had already been made in Judaism during the first century. The citation from 2 Baruch in *The Gospel According to Judas* 10:26 comes from a document that can be dated from the end of first century AD.

xx. CAESAREA PHILIPPI: The town is unknown before the time of Antiochus IV of Syria, but is identified around 200BC as Panion. This name already reflects the cult to Pan that was discovered there. In 20BC Augustus handed over the district to Herod the Great, and after his death it fell into the hands of his son, Philip, who renamed it 'Caesarea' in honour of the Roman Emperor. However, it was known as 'Caesarea Philippi' to distinguish Philip's Caesarea from the beautiful Herodian seaport to the south, the seat of the Roman government at the time of Jesus. This is the name found in the Gospels, including *The Gospel According To Judas* 11. At a later date it reverted to Paneas, and this is the name that is still to be found in the contemporary Arabic word Banias.

xxi. SON OF MAN: This expression, found throughout all four Gospels, is only ever used by Jesus to speak of himself. It is perhaps the clearest indication of Jesus' own understanding of his person and mission. It is an expression that is widely used in Ezekiel to indicate the humble human status of the prophet. It is also found in Daniel 7:13–14. The meaning of the expression in Daniel is widely debated among biblical scholars, especially as Jesus seems to use it in a way that looks back to Dan 7:13–14. It clearly refers to a figure who will overcome all opposition and return in glory. In the Gospels, Jesus also associates the Son of Man with suffering (see Mark 8:31; 9:31; 10:32–34), and some suggest that a suffering Son of Man is already implied by the experience of the people of Israel at the time Daniel was written.

xxii. PETER THE STUMBLING BLOCK: In the Gospel of Matthew, this play upon words using Peter as the stumbling block is very clearly spelt out. The Evangelist reports Jesus' blessing of Peter as 'the rock' (Greek: *petros/petra*) (Matt 16:18). But when Peter tries to prevent Jesus' journey to the cross, Jesus calls him 'Satan' (Aramaic: *satana*) and goes on to explain that this means he is a 'stumbling block' (Greek: *skandalon*).

xxiii. ABBA/FATHER: Jesus spoke Aramaic, and on one occasion in the Gospels (Mark 14:36) he uses the Aramaic word *Abba*, and the Evangelist translates it for his Greek readers as 'father'. The term was used by children who thought of their father in a way that was respectful, obedient and loving.

xxiv. MOUNT TABOR: This small mountain, reached by means of a very steep climb, is located south of Nazareth, on the road to Judea. It is difficult to be certain what actually happened during the strange encounter the disciples have with the transfigured Jesus. It is also impossible to be sure where it took place. The Orthodox traditions generally locate the transfiguration on the more spectacular Mount Hermon. The link and subsequent confusion were inspired by the juxtaposition of Hermon and Tabor in Psalm 89:12: 'The north and the south – you created them; Tabor and Hermon joyously praise your name.'

xxv. JESUS' PASSION PREDICTIONS: Jesus' predictions of his passion during this journey to Jerusalem have developed in the telling. Jesus most likely spoke of his forthcoming death in words very close to: 'The Son of Man will be given into the hands of men and they will kill him.' He probably also spoke, in faith and hope, of his ultimate vindication by God. By the time the Gospels were written, this vindication is expressed in terms of what the early Church believed had actually taken place: resurrection on the third day.

xxvi. THE STRANGER FROM GALILEE: At this point the dependence of *The Gospel According to Judas* on the traditions that formed the Synoptic Gospels (Matthew, Mark and Luke) becomes evident. Jesus comes to Jerusalem for the first time. In the Gospel of John, Jesus is seen regularly in Jerusalem.

xxvii. JESUS AS A PROPHET: Many historical-critical studies of the 'pre-Easter Jesus' have come to the conclusion that Jesus and his disciples understood him to be a prophet.

xxviii. JESUS, SON OF DAVID: Early Christians regarded Jesus as the messianic Son of David (see, for example, Matt 1:1). But in *The Gospel According to Judas*, Jesus does not identify himself with the Son of David. The curing of Bartimaeus is the only occasion in this Gospel where Jesus does not reject the title. It is widely agreed among scholars that the solitary acceptance by Jesus of the term 'Son of David' in the Gospel of Mark (Mark 10:46–52) does not refer to the messianic use of this expression, but to the Jewish tradition that looked back to the historical 'son of David', King Solomon, as a healer. In *The Gospel According to Judas*, Judas misunderstands blind Bartimaeus' appeal to Jesus as a healer. His question of Peter shows that he has renewed hope that Jesus is the Son of David in the sense of being the Davidic Messiah.

xxix. JESUS' ENTRY INTO JERUSALEM: It is difficult to reconstruct what took place, historically, on the occasion of Jesus' entry into Jerusalem. The scene as it is described in *The Gospel According to Judas* depends on John 12:12–16 and Zech 9:9–11.

xxx. SEQUENCE OF EVENTS IN JERUSALEM: In all four Christian Gospels, the sequence of events is exactly the same: entry, preaching, supper, Gethsemane, Jewish trial, Roman trial, crucifixion, burial, discovery of an empty tomb, resurrection appearances (not found in Mark). But the timing of these events varies from gospel to gospel, as it does in *The Gospel According to Judas*.

xxxi. THE SANHEDRIN: This was the highest tribunal permitted by Rome to prosecute and punish Jews according to Jewish laws. It is difficult to determine exactly who made up this body, or even if there was only one Sanhedrin. According to the Gospels, there is one Sanhedrin in Jerusalem, and it is made up of both Priests and Pharisees, along with their Scribes.

xxxii. MONEY DEALERS IN THE TEMPLE: The money dealers who sat in the outer court of the Temple were performing a service essential to the purity of the Temple. It was unlawful to enter the sacred precincts of the Temple carrying any coins that bore the effigy of a human being or an animal. Thus, all who entered the Temple handed over their coins to the money dealers. They exchanged any Jewish money for Tyrian coins, which bore no image. On leaving the Temple, the worshipper would retrieve the money bearing these effigies. This detail must be kept in mind when reading *The Gospel According to Judas* 19:16–19. Jesus is questioned by the Pharisees in the Temple, and asks to see a coin. They show him one bearing the effigy of Caesar. No Jew should have been in possession of such a coin in the Temple.

xxxiii. PASSOVER RITUAL: It is difficult to establish exactly how the Passover was celebrated at the time of Jesus. However, a constant feature found in the various ancient traditions is the use of elements during a meal (bitter herbs, bread and wine) to recall the saving events that are recorded in the biblical account of Israel's exodus from Egypt (see Exodus 12:1–19:26). Jesus repeats these traditions during the last supper, and his action with the bread and wine – along with his words that interpret the meaning of the symbols of bread and wine – remain a constant reminder of the Lord's Supper in most Christian traditions.

xxxiv. THE INNOCENCE OF JESUS: The Christian Gospels (Matthew, Mark, Luke and John) all point out that there was no genuine case against Jesus. The Jewish trial goes ahead on the basis of contradictory evidence, and the Roman trial that follows is punctuated with statements from Pilate emphasizing that he finds no crime in Jesus.

xxxv. INITIATION AT QUMRAN: The indication of a limitation of time that Benjamin can remain at Qumran, unless he wishes to be there for the rest of his life, reflects the evidence of first-century witnesses, Josephus and Philo, along with the texts of the Dead Sea Scrolls. Anyone wishing to join the community was accepted for one year of probation. At the end of that year they were admitted to the ritual bathing that was a key element of Essene practice. Once admitted, the candidate had to remain a further two years, a stay culminating in a ceremony in which an oath of fidelity was taken. Benjamin has no desire to be part of this process, and thus agrees to return to Kerioth.

xxxvi. THE OUTBREAK OF THE WAR: Many factors led to the eventual outbreak of the first Jewish Roman war (also known as the Great Jewish Revolt) in AD66. The crucifixion of anyone who opposed Rome, and the flight and eventual suicide of the Essenes, are reported by the Jewish historian Josephus (*circa* AD37–101). He was a Jew who originally joined the Jewish revolt and fought against the Romans in Galilee, and after he was captured switched allegiance. He is the best witness we have to the events of the Jewish War, although he generally defends the Romans and blames the Jewish zealots for the outcome. The war began under Vespasian (AD66) but Jerusalem was destroyed when Titus was supreme commander of the Roman army (AD70). Both eventually became Emperors of Rome.

xxxvii. TITUS' EDICT: After being surrounded on every side, the leaders of Jerusalem still refused to accept that defeat and destruction were inevitable. Josephus softens Titus' edict, but it is fierce enough: 'Titus was furious that people trapped in their city should demand conditions of him as if they were the conquerors. He ordered that an edict be issued. No longer was anyone to flee the city, nor should they seek any terms for peace. If they attempted to do so, he would not spare them.' (Josephus, *Jewish War*, VI.352)

xxxviii. WATER INTO WINE: It is universally accepted, even by the most critical of scholars, that Jesus performed many miracles in the eyes of his contemporaries, for example, casting out evil spirits and curing the sick. Such events as the walking on the water and the changing of water into wine are generally referred to as 'nature miracles'. As the early Christians began to accept and understand that the risen Jesus was the Christ and the Son of God, they also began to allow traditions to be written into their stories of Jesus that demonstrated that not only YHWH, the God of Israel, was Lord of the sea and master of nature, but so also was Jesus. There is strong Old Testament background to YHWH as master of the elements (Pss 29; 65:7–8; 89:9; 104:3–4; 107:24–32). The coming of the messianic era is also marked by a feast with an abundance of wine and good food (see Hos 2:19–20; Isa 25:6–8; Jer 2:2). However, if it had been true, Jesus would have changed about 120 gallons of water into wine!

xxxix. THE TWELVE: There is widespread agreement that Jesus chose an inner circle of twelve men from among his many disciples and followers. They are known as 'the Twelve' in Matthew, Mark and John. In Luke they become 'the

Twelve Apostles'. Jesus' choice of the Twelve indicated his sense of creating a new people of God built upon the former people of God, founded upon the Twelve Tribes of Israel. The number 'twelve' is theologically significant. The Twelve form the cornerstone for the establishment of God's people. For this reason, once Judas is removed from the group of the Twelve, a further witness to Jesus, from the beginnings to his resurrection, was chosen by lot. The 'Twelve' had to be maintained (Acts 1:21–26).

xl. SUICIDE: There is no explicit commandment against suicide in the Hebrew Bible, but God's primacy over life and Israel's prohibitions on the shedding of human blood imply that it is forbidden. The rabbis eventually came to forbid suicide explicitly. See, for example, the rabbinic teaching in *Genesis Rabbah* 34:21b. It may come as a surprise to some readers of *The Gospel according to Judas* that he did not hang himself. It is popularly accepted by Christians that this was the case. However, there is only one reference to Judas' suicide in the New Testament: Matthew 27:3–10. According to Luke (Acts 1:18), he swelled and burst open in the middle and his bowels gushed out. Nothing is said about the death of Judas in the Gospels of Mark, Luke or John. Thus, only Matthew paints Judas as a Jew whose unforgivable sin of betrayal results in the further sin of suicide. When one becomes aware of the influence of Old Testament texts on Matt 27:9–10 (see Zech 11:12–13; Jer 32:6–15; 18:2–3), it is most likely that Matthew's report of Judas' death is an attempt to further blacken his name, in the light of the Old Testament predictions, when it never actually happened.

xli. THIRTY PIECES OF SILVER: Central to the popular understanding of Judas' betrayal of Jesus is the payment of thirty pieces of silver by the High Priests. No serious New Testament scholar accepts that this ever happened. In the Gospel of Mark, after Judas offers to betray Jesus, it is reported that: 'And when they heard it they were glad, and promised to give him money' (Mark 14:11). The Gospel of Luke does not mention the exchange of any money, nor does the Gospel of John. It should also be noted that the text of the Gospel of Mark does not suggest that any money was ever handed over. The author of the Gospel of Matthew had the Gospel of Mark before him, and he follows most of it, with embellishments. Matthew could not accept that the Messiah would be so easily sold out by this unseemly deal between the priests and one of his disciples. He therefore turns to prophecies from Zechariah and Jeremiah and develops this theme in two major passages: Matthew 26:15 ('And they paid him thirty pieces of silver') and Matthew 27:3–10 (the return of the thirty pieces of silver, Judas' suicide and the purchase of the potter's field with the money). None of this is found anywhere else in the Gospels, but they are the details that have been at the heart of the Christian Church's preaching, and the popular understanding of Judas. Matthew wishes to show that Jesus was not duped. However tragic, the betrayal was the fulfilment of prophecy. The details of the thirty pieces of silver come from Zacheriah 11:12 ('So they weighed out as my wages thirty pieces of silver' [see Matt 26:15]), Zacheriah 11:13 ('So I took the thirty pieces of silver and threw them into the treasury, in the house of the Lord' [see Matt 27:5]), and a collection of texts from Jeremiah 18:2 ('the potter's field' [see Matt 27:7]) and Jeremiah 32:7–9 (the purchase of a field for pieces of silver [see Matt 27:7–9]).

xlii. MASADA: An almost impregnable palace-fortress was built by Herod the Great (*circa* 73–4bc) on the top of a mountain beside the Salt Sea. Even today, it is accessible only by foot from the side of the Salt Sea by what is called 'the snake path'. The Romans, under Titus, eventually overran it in AD74.

xliii. CRUCIFIXION BY TITUS: Crucifixion was regarded by the Romans as the most supreme form of punishment (*summum supplicium*). Josephus reports that Titus used this form of execution regularly during the Jewish War, and especially following the siege of Jerusalem. See, for example, Josephus, *Jewish War*, V.449–451, where Josephus reports the crucifixion of so many Jews each day that 'there was no longer room for the crosses and not enough crosses for the bodies'.

FRANCIS J. MOLONEY

JEFFREY ARCHER

JEFFREY ARCHER is an international best-selling author, with sales of over 125 million copies of such novels as *Kane and Abel*, *The Prodigal Daughter*, *The Eleventh Commandment* and, among his short stories, *The First Miracle*.

He was educated at Oxford and is a former Member of Parliament. He is currently a Member of the House of Lords.

He lives with his wife Mary, at the Old Vicarage, Grantchester, and in London. They have two sons.

PROFESSOR MOLONEY has been a leading figure in the Roman Catholic theological tradition for the past thirty years. For the past eighteen years as a member of the International Theological Commission to the Holy See, he has been closely associated with its chairman, Cardinal Joseph Ratzinger, now Pope Benedict XVI. The author of many studies of the New Testament and its world, his most recent publication is *The Living Voice of the Gospel: The Gospels Today*.

He is currently a major superior of a Roman Catholic religious congregation, the Salesians of Don Bosco.